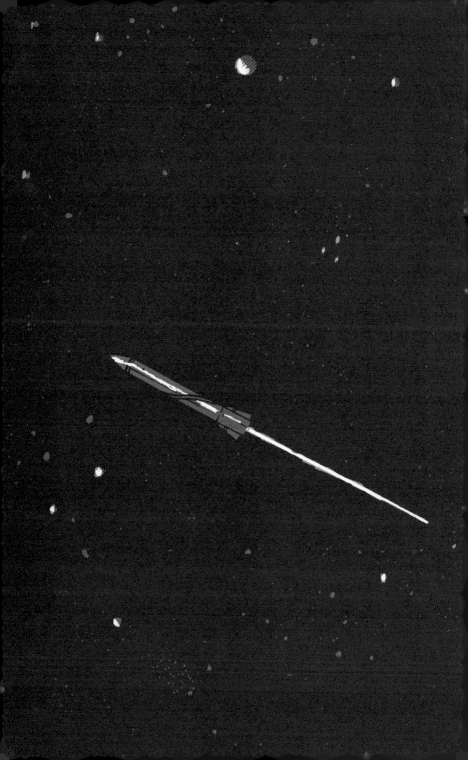

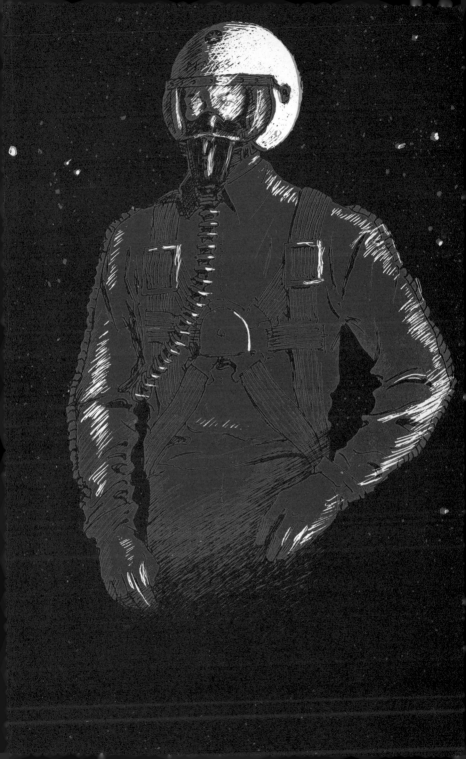

MIKE MARS AT CAPE CANAVERAL

Mike Mars
at Cape Canaveral

BY DONALD A. WOLLHEIM

ILLUSTRATED BY ALBERT ORBAAN

DOUBLEDAY & COMPANY, INC.

GARDEN CITY, NEW YORK

1961

Special Acknowledgment Notice

The author wishes to extend his personal thanks for the valuable assistance rendered him in the course of preparing this book by the United States Air Force. In particular, thanks are due to Major James F. Sunderman, Chief of the USAF Book Program, to Major Kenton D. McFarland and Captain James C. Sparks, Jr., of the USAF Information Office in New York, and to Major Kenneth E. Grine and his staff at Patrick Air Force Base. My gratitude is also due for the hospitality extended to me during my stay in Florida by Mr. and Mrs. William Balter.

Contents

MIKE MARS AT CAPE CANAVERAL

CHAPTER 1

THE MAN FROM SPACE

MIKE MARS could hear the voice giving the countdown. The time was three minutes to go; all was in order. The voice droned on, listing the points to be checked, and faintly Mike could hear the responses in answer. It was a routine affair; nobody anticipated any trouble. It was the scene that spread before Mike's eyes that seemed out of place.

All around him was the quiet blue of the Atlantic Ocean, with no land in sight. The rays of the warm afternoon sun shone down, the sun low in the Maytime sky. The voice was coming from the radio room near the bridge of the destroyer. Mike was standing on the deck nearby.

The United States Navy destroyer *Bayard*, all clean and gray, with the sharp lines of a deadly fighter of the sea, was motionless. A faint bobbing sensation communicated itself to Mike and the others who were passengers that day, but it was a mild and somewhat pleasant sort of motion. Not that Mike would have minded a rough trip. He knew that anyone who was not subject to the dizziness and nausea that comes with the loss of gravity in free-fall space experiments was sure to be free from seasickness.

If there was one thing that their months of experiments had proven, it was that the seven young pilots of Project Quicksilver were all the kind of lucky, healthy, fearless persons who just never would get motion sickness. After all, none of them would have become a qualified commissioned jet pilot had he had that kind of trouble! Much less pass the hard series of tests that resulted in eliminating all the other volunteers for space-flight except the seven of them.

Mike strolled across the iron deck of the ship and rejoined the group of young fellows clustered along it. There were six others there, and as he leaned over and rested his elbows on the rail, one of them, a dark-haired, coppery-featured youth, glanced swiftly at him with keen black eyes. "What's the dope, Mike?" he asked.

"Three minutes" was Mike's reply. Automatically, overhearing him, every one of the other six, as if trained, looked at his wrist watch.

"You must have rehearsed that," said a deep voice behind them. Mike looked back. Colonel Drummond, wearing the blue-gray overcoat of the Air Force, was watching the seven of them from a point near the bridge. With him was another man, in the uniform of a naval lieutenant, one of the ship's officers.

There was a burst of laughter from the seven young men. All looked around at their commander, the head of Project Quicksilver. "But, after all," said Mike laughingly, "why not? We've all been drilled so much in time-reactions it would be strange if we didn't check simultaneously."

"Yep," said his neighbor and best friend, Johnny Bluehawk, the one who had spoken to him first. "It's going to get so that we all sneeze together at the same time."

"Kachoo," exclaimed the tall lanky fellow next in line along the rail. He wore a navy-blue pea jacket rather than the Air Force uniforms of Mike and Johnny. This was Jack Lannigan, Navy pilot and fellow astronaut.

"God bless you," said the one on his right, also in navy blue, a slender young chap with light-brown hair poking out from under his Navy cap. That was Joseph Stacey, the other Navy pilot with the Quicksilver space fliers.

"Don't mention it," said the next in line, Hart Williams, a good-looking young man with close-cropped black hair, who was standing like a handsome movie hero in his Air Force coat.

"Want a handkerchief?" remarked Orin McMahan, red-haired Marine pilot in the greenish jacket, who was next to last in line.

"Minute and a half," coldly commented the stocky, straw-haired Air Force pilot at the end. It was like Rod Harger not to join the fun. Rod was looking at his watch again.

The others fingered the binoculars they wore around their necks and fell silent.

From the open door of the radio shack they could faintly hear the amplified voice from Wallops Island a hundred miles to the west of them, beyond the horizon. "One minute . . ."

Somewhere over there, on a thin sandy stretch of land just off the Virginia coast, a rocket was about to take off. In his mind's eye Mike could see it now. The feat of imagination was really quite easy, for he and the six others had paid a visit to the Wallops Island station of the National Aeronautics and Space Administration, where the rocket firing was now a matter of seconds away.

The rocket would be one of NASA's Little Joe flights. Little Joe was a mighty efficient work horse for practical test flights. It was an all-solid-fuel rocket combination, just about as foolproof as you can get in a large, powerful rocket setup. Solid-fuel rockets were so much easier to handle, having none of the finicky problems presented by the big liquid-fuel rockets with their boiling, sizzling liquid gases.

The Little Joe, as Mike remembered it, was not so little by civilian standards. It stood about fifty feet high and was a cluster of eight powerful solid-fuel boosters, four Pollux-type rockets, and four Recruit rockets. All together they could deliver 250,000 pounds of thrust at launching.

They had been preparing this particular test yesterday when the seven Space Task Group Q astronauts had been there. They had been working on it this morning while the seven had gone aboard the destroyer from their temporary headquarters at Langley, in Hampden, Virginia, and had sailed out of the mouth of Chesapeake Bay up along the coast to this point opposite Wallops.

There was a silence among all those clustered at the destroyer's bow. They could hear the faint voice of the speaker, broadcasting from the blockhouse at the launching site. "Four, three, two, one, go!"

Instinctively all eyes turned toward the horizon. But only blue met their eyes, the blue of the sea and the gray-blue of the horizon. The sun was in their eyes and they squinted against it.

A half hour passed, a half hour of silence and

thought. It would be soon now, Mike thought. "One hundred miles," he murmured to the Cheyenne Johnny Bluehawk next to him.

"A stone's throw," the Indian muttered.

On the ship there was a dragging of ship's ropes, and a glance confirmed that two launches were going down the destroyer's side into the water.

The seven young men, the gray-haired colonel,

Johnny Bluehawk

18

and the naval officer all tilted their heads upward, staring into the sky. They could hear a faint whining sound.

"There she is!" someone cried. Immediately, again as if rehearsed, all seven put binoculars up to their eyes, focused at the tiny dot that had magically appeared in the heavens.

It wasn't the rocket; nobody expected that. The Little Joe rocket had burned itself up after it was about thirty miles out and maybe sixty miles high. The cargo it carried had gone up, riding on momentum; had lifted till it was about a hundred and thirty miles up; and was now coming down on a re-entry orbit not much different than any ballistic missile would take.

But this was no missile. As Mike focused his field glasses he saw it take shape, a small red dot swaying beneath an orange-and-white-striped parachute. It was falling fast, the chute bellying out above it, fighting to slow it down.

He watched, unconsciously tightening his lips. It came into clearer view, a red cone-shaped metallic object, very much in shape like a television master tube.

It was falling more under control, and he followed it down, down, until with a splash it struck the surface of the ocean. There was a small fountain of

"There she is!" someone cried.

water spraying around it; then the parachute fell flat on the surface and floated. The red capsule popped up again instants later, bobbed a bit, then rested gently, rocking lightly like a red fishing float.

Mike Mars leaned over the railing, looking at it. His gray eyes narrowed sharply and for a moment his face screwed up in thought. For an empty capsule, he was thinking, that thing is riding lower in the water than it should.

He remembered having seen a similar capsule floating in the big tank at Langley. Certainly it had bobbed around much higher than this one. He ran a hand through his unruly thatch of sandy hair. Something was not right here.

There was a rumbling sound. Glancing down, he saw that the first of the destroyer's motor launches was moving alongside the ship, just below where he stood. They were preparing to turn and head for the capsule.

"Hey!" suddenly called Johnny. "The thing's opening up!"

Mike looked quickly back at the capsule. Sure enough, the hatch cover at the upper end of the red container, now looking like a buoy, had suddenly popped up. Even as it did so, there was another popping sound, a puff of smoke, and the figure of a man clad in bright-orange flying coveralls popped out of the top like a man shot from a cannon, did a somersault, and hit the water.

"Holy smokes!" Mike shouted. "The ejection seat threw him out. He'll drown!"

While the others leaned over the railing, still astounded by what they had seen, Mike suddenly acted. He glanced down into the water just below him. The launch was still there, the seamen in it apparently just as surprised as the astronauts on deck.

Mike unhesitantly slipped a foot over the railing, climbed over, and, grabbing a rope hanging just below, swung himself down into the launch.

The little boat rocked from the impact of his landing. The shock shook its crew back into action.

"Hurry!" Mike snapped. "He can't swim in that outfit!"

With a roar the launch came to life, turned around, and raced toward the bobbing capsule.

Mike swung himself into the launch.

CHAPTER 2

ALL-OUT AT LANGLEY

MIKE scrambled across the narrow space of the little powerboat and reached the prow. The ensign standing there stepped aside for him. As they drew near the capsule, Mike could see the streak of orange in the water that indicated where the man who had emerged was floating.

"He must be unconscious," said the ensign. "I can't see his head. He's floating, back up, head and legs down."

As the launch roared up to the figure, Mike stripped off his jacket and quickly unlaced his shoes. When the boat had swung about a few feet from the floating body, Mike dived in.

He came up almost under the man. He could see the head hanging limply just under the water. Mike swung an arm under him, quickly lifted him, turned him on his back, and in a few strong strokes hauled him back to the boat.

Willing hands pulled the body from him and helped Mike aboard. From the destroyer came a cheer.

As the launch started back to the *Bayard*, Mike and the ensign leaned over the man they had rescued. Mike was still puzzled. Nothing had been said of a man riding in that capsule. It didn't make sense. This was to be the final feature of the series of experiments and it was to be one of the Project Quicksilver astronauts who would ride inside the capsule. After all, they had been trained for it.

This capsule had indeed come down from the edge of space. If this man, whoever he was, had stowed away inside it, then he had stolen the thunder from the others.

But even as Mike leaned over the silent unmoving figure, his mind refused to accept the possibility. Nobody would have attempted to stow away in the upper escape hatch of that rocket with just a coverall for protection.

The man was heavy—Mike guessed about a hundred and sixty pounds when he had dragged him through the water—and firmly muscled, too.

He gazed down into the stranger's face and gasped. He was looking into a mask, a mask of reddish rubber. There were the vague outlines of a face, eyepits, a nose, closed lips. But it was a mask. Mike ran a hand over it, quickly thrust a hand underneath the wet cloth of the coverall. The man he'd rescued was no man at all! It was a dummy.

When he got back to the ship and the other astronauts found out about it, Mike took a good deal of joshing. But Colonel Drummond seemed rather proud of Mike.

"How could you know they'd put one of their special testing dummies into the capsule? I deliberately didn't tell the fellows about it because I wanted to see their reactions. You did very well, Mike. I'd like to have you on my side if I ever get into trouble!"

Mike laughed with the others. The kidding didn't bother him. "It certainly acted like a man. That dummy was just as heavy and as solidly built as a man. He even felt like a man—the same feel of flesh and muscle and bone."

"That's right," chuckled the colonel. "Those dummies are specially designed to react just like a human body in tests. They were made for testing ejection seats, flying equipment, and other things to be used by real men. The Wallops Island engineers put this one in to test the emergency escape mechanism of the capsule after it came down. You see, it worked."

Springtime in Virginia is as delightful a season as anyone can ask for, and Mike Mars bounded out of bed the next morning full of energy and pep. After dressing quickly, he popped out of his quarters and pounded on the doors of his fellow astronauts. In a matter of minutes all seven of the young fellows were up and looking for breakfast.

The sun was shining down in a cloudless sky and the feel of newly growing things filled the air. Langley Air Force Base was ideally located on the tip of Virginia, bordering the mouth of the Chesapeake in Hampden. Langley was the place where the National Aeronautics and Space Administration maintained the famous Langley Research Center, where so many pioneering studies in aircraft and now astronautics had been made.

Langley had been the home base of the astronauts since the day of their selection. Though all of the seven had spent time visiting various other areas on special missions, they felt that it was here that they would finish their preparations for the conquest of space.

The skilled test pilots who made up the well-publicized group of Project Mercury astronauts were getting their training here, and so the fledgling pilots of the parallel Project Quicksilver assumed that they, too, would continue at Langley. In this they were guessing ahead—and considering that their special group of astronauts was strictly secret, they should have realized that their directors might have other plans.

But Mike Mars wasn't thinking of such things that sunny morning following the naval expedition of the previous day. "What's up for today?" Mike sang out to Johnny Bluehawk as they finished their breakfast.

The young Cheyenne shook his head. "Dunno," he said. "We sort of broke our schedule to go out and work on the X-15."

"You sure did," said Joe Stacey. "While you were away playing with that rocket ship, Hart and Orin and I have really been leaving you in the dust with our space capsule studies. You may have gotten five minutes in outer space with the X-15, Mike, but it's going to be one of us that gets into orbit first. You can just watch our dust!"

Mike laughed. "When you get stranded up there, don't call me to fly up and bail you out!"

"Seriously, though"—Stacey dropped his bantering tone—"we've been doing a lot of work on the space capsule that you'll have to catch up with."

"I guess so," said Mike. "But it doesn't matter at all which of us gets up there first. The thing is the conquest of space. I'll be just as glad if any of us gets up. There's plenty of time for the rest of us to follow. Space flight is only at its dawning and we've all got lots of fruitful years ahead."

Mike glanced up at Rod.

Rod Harger stood up from the table. "Don't forget also that while Columbus discovered America it was named after a fellow who came along twelve years later." As he spoke he thought to himself that Columbus was a fool to let that happen. Now when Harger managed to beat the rest—as he fully intended to do—there'd be no mistake as to who was first and who deserved all the glory.

Mike glanced up at Rod's stocky, straw-thatched figure. "Now that's a fact I hadn't thought of. Just goes to show you we should learn to make haste slowly."

"You'd better learn to make haste hastily," came a new voice, and the seven glanced around to see Colonel Drummond had arrived. "That's the one big difference between us and the Mercury boys. They're going slow, steady, and sure. We're going all out and fast. I'm going to have to stress this more often, though I don't like to dwell on it."

"I think we understand," said Jack Lannigan, who had been with Mike, Rod, and Johnny on the X-15 expedition. "What's the program for today?"

The colonel, who was the director of Space Task Group Q, waved to them to follow him. "Back to our classroom, then, and we'll lay it out. The bus is waiting outside."

The room in which they had been doing their special studies in astronautics looked very much like any classroom in any school around the country. Ever since their arrival at Langley, the seven had been studying there mornings. It was felt that they had to keep up their learning in the things they would need to know as space pilots—things like astronomy, meteorology, the geography of the planet Earth as seen from space, and the mechanics and operations of rocket engines and ballistic flight.

But their task at Langley was not all classroom grind. In the afternoon there had been physical training and, best of all, skin-diving. The pool was big and they had it to themselves during certain hours. There they learned what it would feel like to float easily about without much weight, to direct themselves through the green water in face mask and "SCUBA" outfit with a gentle kick that would move them swiftly about the alien substance. Adjusting their muscles to the lesser weight of their bodies was an important thing. Next to actual weightlessness, it was the best training they could get for handling themselves in the space between planets.

Mike loved that part of it—as they all did. There had been some terrific games played under water, and they had devised some fast and exciting variations on water sports. It was even fun when they had been given puzzles to put together under water!

There had also been other training work. For instance, they had all mastered the F-100 Super Sabres even before their selection as Quicksilver astronauts. And during the time they had been at Langley, all of them had visited other Air Force bases and had acquired experience in the F-102 Interceptor and the F-104 Starfighter.

In addition, Mike and three of the seven had gone to Edwards Air Force Base in California, where they had studied the mastery of a rocket-driven plane and where Mike had piloted the X-15, the world's first real spaceship, up into outer space.

After the seven had taken their seats, Colonel Drummond went to the front desk, waited for them to hear him.

They all came to attention. The gray-haired colonel glanced at Mike briefly, then looked at each of the others. "Time is pressing," he said, and halted. The seven leaned forward.

"We have reason to believe that another country is preparing to put a man in orbit sooner than we had expected. Therefore, we are cutting short our work here. We are going to begin the next active stage of our program in advance of our plans. The space capsule is ready. Seven of these capsules have already been secretly delivered to Cape Canaveral. A stock of Redstone rockets has also been put in readiness

Colonel Drummond stressed the importance of time.

there. In ten days' time the first one of you is going to ride into space atop one of those rockets. The rest of you will follow as fast as the experiments can be set up!"

CHAPTER 3

THE BEARDED SCIENTIST

THERE WAS a general gasp at the news. All seven had known of their schedule months ago when they had first been briefed on the plans for America's man-in-space program—both the public Mercury one and that of their own secret Quicksilver group. But somehow it was different then, when the dates were sometime in the uncertain future, from now, when a date was suddenly advanced. Ten days—that meant only a week and a half away!

Mike raised a hand. The colonel nodded to him. "Excuse me, sir, isn't this a little too soon for some of us? I know that three of us have been working on the capsule and its mechanism—McMahan, Stacey, and Williams—but the rest of us missed several weeks while we were mastering the problem of the X-15."

Colonel Drummond frowned. "That's quite true. You and the others who were out at the Air Force

Flight Testing Center are not fully ready to ride the capsule. You will be expected to continue your studies on it, to train more before you can undertake the task of riding into outer space.

"But the three you mentioned are just about ready. They've studied the capsule, they've gone out to St. Louis to the McDonnell aircraft plant where the capsules are being made, and they've observed it from start to finish. They've seen many more testings of the capsule and miniature models than you have.

"Because of the speed-up of our program, our urgency to get into space, we are going ahead with the tests, placing those three first in order. The flights will be about one week apart. That gives you others more than a month to catch up with the capsule knowledge the first three already have."

He picked up a sheet of paper, looked it over. "I have here the schedule for the Redstone rockets. The first to attempt the flight will be Hart Williams. After him, Joseph Stacey will go up. Next will come Orin McMahan. By that time, we trust the remaining four will be brought up to date.

"Following McMahan will come Rod Harger. After that, in order, will come Samson, Lannigan, and Bluehawk."

Mike Mars, whose full name was Michael Alfred Robert Samson but who was better known as Mike

Mars because his initials spelled out M.A.R.S., was not upset by the fact that he would not be the first in the rocket rides. He had had his chance with the X-15: he had carried out the first excursion into the airless void beyond the atmosphere of Earth at the controls of that first of all spaceships.

He took the news calmly, but the rest of the fel-

Mike Mars

lows were quite excited. Rod Harger sat silent, deep in his own private thoughts. Bluehawk and Lannigan just grinned and went over and began slapping the first three on the back.

"Bring home a hunk of vacuum for me," said Jack Lannigan to handsome Hart Williams.

"Yes," added Johnny Bluehawk, "and if you see any meteors, pick up one for me for luck."

Williams smiled, proud and yet just a little scared. In a week and a half, he thought, I'll be up there on top of all that blazing explosive, going up into space with nothing around me but the thin shell of that little bottle we call the capsule. But then he braced himself—I'm ready, he thought further, I'm ready.

Redheaded Orin McMahan and slender Joe Stacey were beaming also. They'd go; they had not had the chance to get at the X-15, but now they were going to get repaid for their loss.

Mike did feel excited about the coming flights. It was good to know that action was coming fast. He hated to have to idle around waiting. Waiting was a difficult thing, and in its own way it could take the spirit out of a fellow just as much as failure could. Yet the best things in life were to be had often by just such waiting. If a chance could be bettered by patience, then patience was a virtue that had to be learned. . . .

Mike had trained himself as a boy to concentrate on learning whatever was needed to master a situation. It was one of his rules, and he never allowed himself to depart from it.

As a boy Mike had read of the planets and the stars. It was then that he had resolved to be among those who would explore them. Mainly he had dreamed as a boy, both in grammar school and in high school, of the red planet, the Earth's neighbor outward from the sun, the mysterious world of Mars.

Mars excited him with its mystery and its wonder. He had read in the astronomy books about the only other planet known to man that astronomers were sure harbored living things. True, the astronomers would admit only that they were sure that some kind of vegetable life lived there—most probably only some low hardy form, such as moss or mountain lichens, or perhaps some tough type of desert plants. But life—any kind of life—was a wonderful thing.

Mike had always felt that where there was plant life, there might well be animal life. And where animal life, why not intelligent life? He didn't know, but he wanted to learn. Hadn't such great astronomers as Percival Lowell and William Pickering believed in the possible existence of higher forms of Martian lives? Lowell, for instance, thought that the Martians had a very high civilization based on the marvelous engineering of a world-wide system of canals that carried the water from the frozen poles to the planet's arid equator.

The canals had been a source of disbelief by students of the ruddy planet for many years after Lowell. But now their existence was again accepted. There *were* thin spidery lines crisscrossing the desert planet, running from pole to pole! Mike, who had read everything he could get his hands on about Mars, knew that there were still many opinions about these lines and that most astronomers still did not accept Lowell's conclusion that the canals were actually the waterways of an intelligent society.

Mike wanted so very much to know that he had pledged his life to the conquest of space. He would direct his life to becoming a space flier, to going out, to going finally to Mars to see for himself.

From the moment that he, as a boy of twelve, had come to this decision, he had laid out rules for the conduct of his life. The first had been to keep himself in good health, in good strength, never to abuse his body by laziness or indulgence, never to poison himself by excessive drinking or smoking.

The second had been to master his studies, to learn new things fast and correctly, and always to keep his mind open for further knowledge. Science and arithmetic were the tools of a space flier, so to those he gave special application.

The third had been never to lose faith with himself. No matter what disappointment came, or what hardship, he must believe unyieldingly that he could and would get to Mars.

He had made another decision, too, and that was that the career of a pilot in the Air Force was the one that would lead most directly to space flying.

So Mike had trained himself and found that by persistence and determination his ambition was coming true, step by step. He had utilized his initials M.A.R.S. to keep his goal before him—on his school books, on his sports equipment, on the glider he had flown one summer during high school vacation, on the planes he had learned to fly for the Air Force. . . .

The colonel tapped for the astronauts' attention. "Gentlemen," he said, "we are not through."

As the seven quieted down, the door of their room opened and three people came in. Two of them were men; one was not. The eyes of the seven young pilots settled at first on this third party.

It was a girl, a young girl, perhaps about seventeen, Mike thought. She was pretty, with sparkling blue eyes and glistening black hair. Wearing a black skirt and green blouse, she slipped quietly into a seat in a corner of the room.

All eyes turned just as swiftly away from her and leveled on the two men. One they knew. This was the famous German space medicine expert, Dr. Hugo Holderlin. They had all worked with him, for he had alternated with the colonel as the head of their studies and working program.

The other man was a newcomer but one who instantly commanded their attention. He was a big man dressed in civilian clothes. He had a short black beard and mustache and hair as black as the girl's. His eyes, too, were twinkling blue. Father and daughter, thought Mike—there is a resemblance.

He must have been in his fifties. There was an air of quiet strength about him that caused a feeling of immediate respect. He was smiling calmly as he nodded to Colonel Drummond and shook hands.

Then the stranger and Dr. Holderlin drew up chairs and sat down near the colonel, facing the group of astronauts.

Colonel Drummond looked around at the seven young men. "You all know Dr. Holderlin. You know that he's been associated with Project Quicksilver from the start as I have. Now allow me to introduce the third member of Space Task Group Q, with whose appointment our little organization is completed and ready for action.

"This is Dr. Merlin Van Ness. Dr. Van Ness is a member of the National Aeronautics and Space Administration. You have probably heard of his work

Dr. Van Ness   Dr. Hugo Holderlin

in connection with a number of projects having to do with rockets and space flight.

"The directorate of Project Quicksilver will consist from now on of the three of us—Dr. Van Ness representing the civilian authorities, Dr. Holderlin representing space medicine and research, myself on behalf of the armed forces. The manpower of Project Quicksilver will consist of you seven.

"Our permanent headquarters will be established at Dr. Van Ness's private estate in Florida, which is appropriately named Skyhook. We are going to leave Langley for Skyhook tomorrow morning. The need for security is great. We all know that attacks have been made on some of you astronauts. We know that though our existence is a secret, there are enemies who have learned of us who will stop at nothing to destroy our hopes.

"Skyhook is close enough to Cape Canaveral to allow us to get speedy action and yet it is secluded enough for us to achieve the security we need and the secrecy we desire."

CHAPTER 4

STARFIGHTER HAZARD

MIKE MARS shot a quick glance across at Johnny Bluehawk. The young man caught his glance, nodded. Yes, this was the Dr. Van Ness they had heard of. Mike looked back at the bearded man with interest.

He knew that many of the decisions made to advance America's space flight program had been the work of this eminent scientist and business wizard. One of the men who had grown up with the age of aviation, who had sponsored and suggested many of the improvements that made the airplane come of age during the twenties and thirties of this century, Dr. Van Ness had been an early and ardent supporter of the rocket program and an outspoken advocate of space flight.

Mike had read of him in many popular articles. He remembered one piece that Dr. Van Ness had written while Mike was still in high school. It had made

45

a deep impression on him then as a result of the scientist's brilliant arguments in favor of the belief that space-flight was a possibility in the near future although there were many then, in the days before Sputnik, who pooh-poohed the idea.

Mike knew that Merlin Van Ness had been rewarded for his determined belief in the future of aviation by having become a millionaire several times over when his belief turned into reality. He also knew that he was a big influence in the NASA program. But it was a thrill to learn that Project Quicksilver must have been one of his special ideas—and that now he would personally take a hand in its development.

Colonel Drummond's words cut into Mike's thoughts. "I will not ask Dr. Van Ness to say anything to you now. You will all have plenty of opportunity to speak with him yourselves as we move into high gear. There will be no assignments for the rest of this day. I want you to report here tomorrow morning bright and early, packed and ready to travel. We will have planes ready for us then."

He stepped down and the session was over. The seven young fellows rose from their desks startled and excited by the developments. It was close to lunch time and they started out of the room to make their way across to the airmen's cafeteria nearby.

As Mike was about to go out the door, the bearded scientist put out a hand and grasped his arm. "Hold on, Lieutenant Samson," he said. "I want to congratulate you on your handling of the X-15. I've been going over the tapes on the flight and you did a fine job."

Mike swung about and, a little abashed, took the proffered hand. "Why, it was nothing, sir," Mike said with a shy smile. "The plane was in perfect shape, thanks to the engineers, and all I had to do was just follow instructions."

"Nonsense," said Van Ness, "I know better. It took guts to carry that through, and the tapes showed you never flinched. Why, blast it, I'd have been scared to do it myself, even if I were your age and in condition."

Mike shook his head. "I can't believe that, sir," he said. "If you're the man I've read about, you'd have done it better. I've read some of your writings and I've read about your record. You've—you've been sort of a hero to me."

The bearded scientist beamed, then slapped Mike on the back. "I only wish I could have visited outer space, even for the few minutes you did. I'm afraid that I'm too old for the great events to come, but by gosh I aim to be in the gallery cheering."

Mike was beginning to feel uncomfortable. He

47

didn't like to be flattered, even when he knew it was sincerely given as in this case. He felt strongly that the man who happened to pilot a space craft was just the end man of a long team of hard-working, ardent men, every one of whom deserved the same applause. Dr. Van Ness sensed this in Mike and, taking the young pilot by the arm, drew him around.

"I'd like you to meet another Van Ness who's in your cheering gallery. This is my little girl Vivian," he said. Mike found himself face to face with the black-haired girl he had already suspected of being the scientist's daughter.

Vivian, whose blue eyes were fixed excitedly on Mike, suddenly flushed and turned to her father. "Daddy," she said in an embarrassed tone, "I'm *not* a little girl any more and I wish you wouldn't say that."

The scientist guffawed. "Oh, I'm sorry. She's a big girl now. All of seventeen and in junior college besides."

Vivian was plainly irritated. "You're impossible, Dad," she said, and then turned suddenly on Mike. "Let's get out of here where we can talk sensibly. Besides, I promised the other girls in my class to bring back some autographs of the astronauts. Maybe you can help me."

Mike began to feel himself trapped. He looked

"I'm not *a little girl!*" Vivian said.

about to see if any of the other astronauts were around to help him out of his predicament. He saw Johnny's broadly smiling face turned toward him as he was rapidly exiting down the corridor—and every one of the others had also successfully made a getaway.

So Mike had to play the gentleman, much as he would rather have joined his friends. He went out of the building with the chattering girl hanging on his arm, and he promised her he'd try to round up some of the Project Mercury men's autographs.

"But you can't have mine and my friends', you know, because we're top secret. . . . How—incidentally—did you know of our work?" he said to Vivian.

"Don't you think Daddy talks about it at the dinner table?" she said. "I know it's secret, but I'm in on it. After all, you and the others are going to be staying and working on Daddy's estate. And when I'm home from school, that's where I stay. You'll like it —it's big, and the grounds are lovely, and we have our own private flying field, and I already know how to fly a light plane myself, and I'm going to get a license just as soon as Daddy can arrange it, and we've a lake all our own, and you can do skin-diving there, and——"

"Hey, wait a minute, one thing at a time," Mike said. Good heavens, he thought, what did I do to deserve this? "If you know so much, do you know what kind of plane we're going down to Skyhook in tomorrow?"

"Of course I do," she said. "It's a Douglas C-47. Perfectly dull old DC-3 ship, and we'll go to Orlando and drive from there to Skyhook, which is a couple of dozen miles away. I'm hungry. Why don't we find some place to eat?"

Mike flinched. Maybe he could figure out some way of not getting stuck with her for several hours in a prop-driven "Gooney Bird." Maybe there was a plane he could borrow and fly down himself. "Excuse me," he said, "but I have to see someone at Base Operations. You go ahead to the cafeteria and I'll meet you there."

Vivian bit her lip in disappointment. "Oh, all right," she said. "But be sure you come."

Mike hastily set off toward Base Operations, mentally thanking his stars and hoping he would have some luck. To his delight, his hunch was right. When he asked around at the Operations building, he ran into a major who happened to be looking for a couple of pilots with time on their hands.

"There are two planes that have to be delivered to Tyndall Air Force Base in Florida. That's on the Gulf Coast, and I'm sure you could get a pickup there for Orlando. We've a pair of F-104 Starfighters waiting for someone to take them down there. If you can fly one of them, then I'll only have to find one other pilot to take the other."

"Wow!" said Mike. "That's my dish. I've handled the Starfighters and they're beauties. I know just the man to take the other one down," he added, thinking that Johnny Bluehawk would jump at the chance also.

"O.K.," said the major, "they'll be fueled, checked out, and waiting for you at nine tomorrow."

Mike left him in high spirits and made his way quickly to the cafeteria, forgetting in his excitement that his "admirer" was waiting for him there. As it happened, she didn't bother him, because she was seated at a table with Hart Williams and the grinning bean pole Jack Lannigan and was pumping them with questions, to which they were replying with amused tolerance.

Johnny Bluehawk was delighted to hear what Mike had arranged. Rod Harger and Orin McMahan, seated at the same table, shook their heads. "Some guys have all the luck," said the marine.

Rod narrowed his eyes, looked thoughtful. "Maybe I can arrange something, too," he said. "I have a chance to meet my father in Washington tonight if I can get up there this afternoon. Maybe I can raise a jet for myself in that area."

Mike fell to on his meal. He had the luck at that, he thought. But he didn't know just how his luck would play tricks on him. For when he turned up at the field the next morning, along with Johnny, and they walked out to the two glistening silver and orange Starfighters waiting for them, so long and slim and speedy in appearance, there was a third person standing by the ladder leading into the cockpit of Mike's plane. This person, like Mike, was dressed in an Air Force coverall and G-suit, was wearing a white high-altitude helmet and carrying an oxygen mask. As Mike came up, holding his own white helmet with its neatly initialed M.A.R.S. on the brim, he wondered who this pint-sized aviator in the baggy bulky suit was.

"Hi, there!" said the other person, and in a flash Mike's heart sunk through his shoes. "I'm going along with you as a passenger. I found out it was a two-seater, an F-104B, and I got Daddy to agree to my going along. I always wanted a chance to fly faster than sound, and Daddy says you're one of the best pilots on the Quicksilver team. Gee, isn't it exciting! How high do you plan to go?"

"Now look here, Miss Van Ness," Mike started to argue, but she waved a thickly gloved hand and started up the ladder. "It's all right, I tell you. I have Dad's official permission, so you've got nothing to worry about. If I make you nervous, I'll stay quiet as a cat and you won't even know I'm around."

She climbed into the narrow confines of the rear seat and began to fasten the buckles of her oversized helmet. Mike glanced at the wide grins on the faces of the ground crew men watching him, swallowed hard, and climbed up without another word and took his place in the front cockpit.

A little distance away, another Starfighter, a single-seater, began its roaring jets. Johnny was moving for the take-off. Mike turned on his jets, waved for the crew release, called to the tower.

In five minutes the two fast planes were hurling themselves into the upper atmosphere under the impulses of their superbly powerful fighter-interceptor jets. Vivian was true to her promise: Mike had not heard a word from her, but he grinned as he heard her suck her breath in from the force of the terrific acceleration when he threw in his afterburners for the fast rise. If he had a mind to, he could give her one ride that should satisfy her thirst for flying thrills for a long time.

Though Mike was really much too nice a fellow to carry through that thought, the decision was to be taken out of his hands very shortly. For it would indeed be a ride neither occupant of the F-104B would soon forget.

CHAPTER 5

THE PHANTOM VOODOO

"SEE THAT your oxygen mask is well adjusted," Mike said on the intercom that supplied the only means of communications between pilot and passenger. "I'm rising to 40,000 feet."

He couldn't see her in the back seat and he wasn't going to try to look. But her voice came back a little breathless, he thought. "Oh, I've got it on tight. I know how. Daddy taught me once back at home. Is 40,000 all you can go up to? I was told these planes could go up twice that height, maybe more."

Mike kept his eyes on his instruments and grinned to himself. So she wanted height and speed, did she? Just for that he'd fly as low and as slow as he could safely, considering how powerful the Starfighter was.

A voice came on his radio earphones. "Mars 2 to Mars 1. What's the flight course, Mike?"

That was Johnny, flying somewhere ahead of him and possibly higher. Their old code names when they were on the training team in their jet pilot student days was the Mars number. Mike had been the leader of that team of four and their instructor had given the whole group the name from his initials on his training jet.

"Mars 1 to Mars 2," Mike called back. "You set your own course. I'll see you at Tyndall an hour later. A load of eggs, Johnny, a load of eggs."

He hoped his friend would understand what he meant. When a plane "had a load of eggs," that would have ordinarily meant a load of bombs; but Johnny knew the Starfighter was not a bomber, though it could carry missiles and rocket weapons when in action. Johnny knew perfectly well that Mike was not flying a plane that was armed. So by the load of eggs Mike hoped he'd catch on that the girl in the back seat was going to be handled with care and caution.

There was a wait, and then he heard his radio beam hum. Johnny's voice came over singsongy: "Rock-a-bye baby . . . on the sky hop . . . when you go gently, the cradle won't bop." There was a pause. "See you . . ."

The radio cut off. Mike was holding the plane at 40,000. He held his hand on the throttle of his powerful jets until the plane was purring along at about

400 miles an hour, far below supersonic speed. He intended to hold it at that all the way.

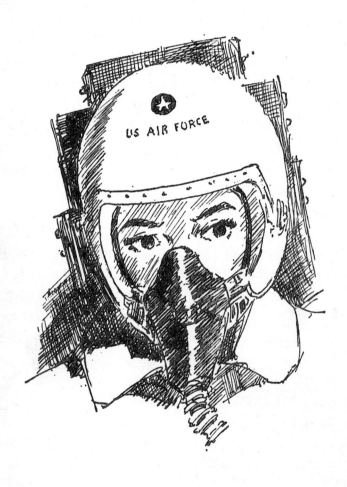

Vivian chattered over the intercom.

"Can't you go any faster?" said Vivian, sounding a little irritated on his earphones. "Really, you mustn't be worried on my account. Why, I've been flying in planes since I was ten years old, and I do know all about planes, but I've never flown faster than sound and I'm so excited . . ."

Mike leaned forward, flicked a switch on his controls, cutting off communication inside the plane. He'd go mad if he had to listen to those endless questions and explanations. Not that he didn't think she was a perfectly nice girl, but, after all, when a fellow flies a plane, he wants to be quiet with his thoughts. Enough was enough.

They flew on in peace and silence for about half an hour. He called ahead once, setting his course again with the ground control at Macon, Georgia, then flicked off. Below, they crossed from sunlit ground into clouded territory, and the ship moved straight and calmly like a silver dart in the clear blue above the white fluffy tops of a carpet of clouds.

What Vivian Van Ness was saying or thinking, Mike didn't know or care. He loved flying, and as a fighter-pilot-turned-astronaut he enjoyed the great feeling of calm that it gave him to be alone in the heavens, far above the noise and conflict of the earth, up near the stars he loved so well, alone with his dreams of space and the future.

It would have been nice, he reflected, if he could have pushed the Starfighter all out to its ceiling and real speed, much faster than sound, but . . .

By this time Johnny must be hundreds of miles away, and if there were any other planes around, he could not see them. He looked down, over the edge of the cockpit, at the white cloud bank below.

He squinted. There *was* a moving dot down there, come to think of it! A plane, and evidently rising up toward him.

It was still quite far away, Mike thought. He turned his attention to the controls a moment, then looked down and ahead. The plane was rising very swiftly now, and it was definitely a jet and a fast one.

He watched it with caution. It looked Air Force or at least Navy, he thought, for it was silvery and certainly had the suggestion of a fighter. What was it?

He lifted the Starfighter slightly, swung it aside a bit. That plane seemed headed for him much too directly. What kind of a clown was flying that plane anyway? Mike had heard that some fighter pilots on maneuvers took risks out of sheer playfulness. Could this be such a character?

The plane was coming at him, he thought. Or, no, it might just pass him by. He could see it quite clearly now. It was a Voodoo jet, the F-101, and Air Force too by its orange color marks. Must have come from some base, and it's looking me over.

If this was to be a game of chicken, I'm going to hold. Let him try and scare me, he thought.

Mike held the Starfighter on course, determined not to increase his speed or height. The other plane was in clear sight now, tearing at him. With a roar it passed him by in a split second and the F-104 slipped through its trail of smoke. That fellow plays too close, Mike thought. He reached to flick on his radio, call the ground or get the pilot and tell him to call the game off.

But then he saw the Voodoo swerve around and head back. Mike pulled back his control, lifted the speedy ship's nose to bring his plane up fast. That crazy pilot was definitely trying to scare him. Playing games, Mike thought. Two can play at that, but I'll find out who you are.

The Voodoo came tearing back like a hawk swooping on its prey. There came a flash of light from under one of its wings. A trail of black smoke raced away in front of it. Mike gasped, slammed his stick back.

The Starfighter shot upward, zooming away. That was a rocket missile, Mike thought in astonishment. That man is firing at me!

He saw the point of white that was the missile streak past below him—a miss. Even as Mike

61

climbed, he saw that the Voodoo had adjusted its speed to his and was climbing right after him. Looking back, he again saw a spark from the other wing. A second missile!

Mike turned his attention to his controls. He slammed on his extra power and the Starfighter surged ahead violently under terrific acceleration. Mike was shoved back in his seat, but he had trained for this. He hoped Vivian wasn't hurt by the sudden burst of speed, but she'd be hurt worse if that rocket caught them.

Up the plane roared, and Mike swung it around, swung it back and forth, even as he climbed. The rocket would miss him. He could go faster than the rocket if he wished, and he did.

Within seconds the F-104B must have crashed the sound barrier, for Mike could no longer feel the thrumming of the jets. There was a tension and a silence within the cockpit. He climbed higher and higher.

Glancing back, he saw the Voodoo begin to lose distance. It was a fast ship, by gosh, supersonic too, and a devil, but it wasn't the equal of the Starfighter, and Mike was going to prove it. He knew he'd better or he'd never return to tell the tale. Whoever that was, he meant business.

Mike clenched his teeth. Another rocket was

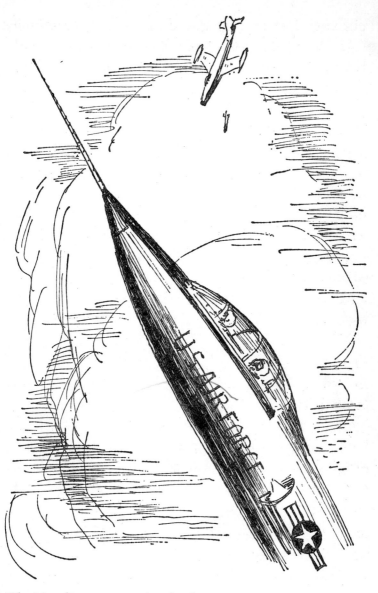

The Voodoo came tearing back.

streaking after him now, and his plane was already at Mach 1.5. Must be 1000 miles an hour now and about 70,000 elevation. The Voodoo was left behind: it couldn't make that height—but maybe the rocket could. The rocket missile, after all, had the speed of the plane when it started and was rising faster on its own. The very same principle, Mike thought, of the second stage of a space rocket leaving the first stage behind.

That brought to mind himself and his own mission. He kept his eyes glued on his dials now, and as he did so he whispered a little poem that he had first made up as a boy in school and that always came back to him in moments of great peril:

Michael Mars is my name.
America's my nation.
Space-flying is my game
And Mars my destination!

Faster and faster. Mach 2, and the needle was hovering, quivering at that point. The altimeter read 90,000 feet. Mike leveled off, shot forward like a lightning bolt. He glanced back and down. There was no plane in sight. No rocket missile either. Nothing. Below, the ground was a distant lake of white—just the tops of clouds miles below. The horizon stretched far. He could see the outlines of the Great

Smokies hundreds of miles away, pushing through the clouds that covered the southland that morning.

Twice the speed of sound and maybe eighteen miles up. The sky was visibly darker up here. He held the speed, realizing that the plane was eating up fuel at a much faster rate up here where the air was so thin. At this speed he'd be at Tyndall the same time as Johnny.

He thought suddenly of his passenger. She must be scared stiff. Maybe she was injured by the quick speed. Maybe she had fainted from fear of the attacking plane. Good gosh, he'd better find out!

He flicked on the intercom. "Miss Van Ness," he said. "Are you all right?"

Instantly her voice came back. It sounded gay and excited. "Oh, Mike," she said. "That was so much fun. Isn't this thrilling! I didn't think you were ever going to go all out, but you did, and did it just to please me! Oh, Mike, wait'll I tell the girls at school about this. Twice the speed of sound and so high! It's . . . it's just dreamy!"

He flicked off the intercom and groaned. "Dreamy!" he muttered. "My gosh, I bet she never even saw that Voodoo!"

CHAPTER 6

THE RED SPEEDSTER

HE SLOWED the plane, brought it closer to the ground. He had filed a flight plan according to rules before taking off, and now he would have to inform ground control of the alteration and his new location. He hesitated about informing them of the strange attack.

If the girl in the back seat had seen the mysterious Voodoo and its rocket missiles, he would have to inform ground authorities at once. If she had not seen it, how could he prove what had happened? Again there was the question of the secrecy of Project Quicksilver to consider. Send an alarm and there would be a big outcry and inquiry from all sorts of Air Force and civilian control agencies as to the why and wherefore. How could he explain what had happened without breaking secrecy?

Hesitantly, he spoke to Vivian. "Did you happen

to notice that plane that was following us a few minutes ago?"

Her voice bubbled back. "What plane? I was too
utterly thrilled watching the speedometer back here
and I really didn't look around. Was there a plane?
What kind was it? I'll bet you outdistanced it so
fast . . ."

He switched off again, shook his head. She'd never
noticed the attack. Well, that settled it. He'd keep
this quiet until he could report it in confidence to the
colonel or Dr. Van Ness. Let them try and track it
down through the secret channels open to them.

The rest of the trip was smooth and without inci-
dent. In almost no time at all the superfast jet found
itself curving around beyond the coast of the Gulf of
Mexico, sweeping down lower to bring itself into the
wide grassy fields of Tyndall Air Force Base, located
on the northwestern edge of Florida. Down Mike
swooped, low over the wide runways, popped his
drag parachute as his wheels touched, and rolled to
a stop. He taxied in to the field and brought the
F-104B to a stop alongside a group of similar Starfighters lined up and ready for action as part of America's all-weather around-the-clock defense forces.

Mike and Vivian stomped into Base Operations
together, holding their helmets and masks in their
hands. Mike noticed out of the corner of his eye that

Vivian was a bit wobbly in the knees and that she was strangely silent. In fact, he saw her bang her ear several times with the palm of her hand as if to stop its ringing. It was a common effect of first flights at such speeds and altitudes, and if her ear was ringing in protest, well, she could talk about that, too, back at school.

Actually he didn't want to be mean about it. She seemed like a good sport, but he wished in a way that she had seen that Voodoo attacker. It would have made his story more believable when he finally told it.

He ran into Johnny Bluehawk coming out the locker room. Johnny stopped short when he saw him, looked at him in amazement.

"What happened to the crate of eggs, Mike? You must have sure speeded up delivery!"

Mike laughed. "I sure did. Come on back while I get out of these togs and let me tell you something."

Johnny came back into the locker chamber, and while Mike took off his heavy flying clothes he told him about the attack. The swarthy young pilot's eyes darkened and for a moment his face grew very fierce. "Somehow," he said, "I see Rod Harger behind this."

Mike looked at him sharply. "Rod? I dunno. It

seems a little strong for him. It must have been Cahoon again, still trying to 'get' me."

Johnny frowned. "Cahoon? Wherever he is or whatever he's doing, I can't believe that he could get hold of a Voodoo jet fighter so easily. But Rod might. Besides, remember that Rod excused himself from coming down with the others. He said he went to Washington. He might have gone to some other base, told some cock-and-bull story, and borrowed a Voodoo. Or just took it on false identification. It would take a well-trained pilot to handle one of those—and he had to work fast."

Mike shook his head. "Rod Harger's a strange fellow," he said slowly, "but I just can't believe he'd be doing things like this. I know you've been suspecting him of dirty work from the beginning, but it's just too much. Besides, nobody has ever connected him with Cahoon and his doings. What Cahoon's motive is, I can't figure, but it could be connected with some personal vengeance against the Air Force, or maybe he's got some hopes of selling himself to some enemy of our country. But I couldn't accuse Rod of a thing like this."

His best friend was still frowning. "I'm going to try to find out just where Harger was today and how he gets down to Skyhook, or says he did. I think that you're just too decent a guy, Mike, to believe how rotten some people can get for the sake of self-glory."

At that moment, Vivian called in. "Hey, you fellows, are you ever going to come out of there and let me get out of these hot coveralls? If you'll hurry, the nice colonel out here says he can get us a flight to Orlando in an hour. As passengers in a comfy transport. That should give us time to have some lunch. And I'm just famished!"

Mike and Johnny exchanged pained glances. "You must admit," whispered Johnny, "that she has a persuasive way with her, lining up the colonel and all. I guess we'll just have to be gentlemen and play nursemaid the rest of the way."

"After her, going into space will be a pleasure," murmured Mike. "It may prove to be the only place we can go to get away from her!"

Ten minutes later found the three of them eating lunch in the pleasant quarters of the Officers Club. The swaying palms of the Gulf Coast, the balmy winds from the wide waters, and the warm air of Florida began to work their charm. Mike felt rested and calm and banished his concern about the mysterious attacker from his mind. The girl chattered on; the two pilots let her talk, listened with only half an ear, and managed to enjoy themselves.

Fifty minutes later they were back on the field

again, climbing into a light transport plane as passengers.

Another hour later, after a comfortable flight on cushioned seats over the broad blue waters of the Gulf of Mexico and the green and brown stretches of central Florida, the plane deposited the two astronauts and the vivacious Vivian at McCoy Air Field near Orlando, central city of Florida's orange-growing district.

As they walked over to the parking lot, hoping that there would be a car waiting for them, Vivian suddenly clapped her hands. "Oh, look!" she said. "Daddy had one of his men drive my car over and leave it for us. See it? The bright-red speedster there at the corner of the lot."

She started running toward it, and the two young fellows trotted after her. It was a nice car—a trim, low-slung, and speedy little sports car, painted a brilliant scarlet with red leather seats. Vivian had reached it first and was sliding into the driver's seat.

"Oh no," said Mike, "not that. Maybe one of us had better drive."

"Don't be a square," said Vivian. "I know the road and I can drive. Are you great big supersonic pilots afraid of a little tiny four-wheeled bucket of bolts and a girl driver?"

Johnny and Mike looked at each other and

71

shrugged. They gingerly eased themselves into the crowded space of the front seats, and Mike crossed his fingers and held them up for Johnny to see. With a sudden roar of an unmuffled engine, Vivian gunned the little speedster forward and they shot off, going faster every minute.

The only advantage of the mad ride, Mike thought afterwards, was that the car was too noisy and the wind of their motion too violent for the girl to attempt conversation. Instead, he and his friend simply gripped their seats, resigned themselves to the worst, and held on for dear life. Riding a jet plane was nothing, he felt, compared to tearing along narrow back-country roads, through Florida pine forests with their hanging Spanish moss, past little lakes, past orange groves, through tiny towns, all at breakneck speed with a young girl at the wheel evidently determined to show her two aviators that she also could smash speed limits.

Mike supposed, as he watched the road unfold before him, that Vivian was trying to get one more thrill out of the trip, for she would surely be on her way back to school the next day.

After a wild, roaring ride, the little red car suddenly came tearing up a narrow side road and jammed to a jolting stop just inches away from a gate in a mesh wire fence that cut across the road. Vivian jumped out, opened the gate with a key. "This is Skyhook," she said, "and I think you'll like it."

"We will if you'll just slow down the rest of the way," said Mike laughingly. She threw him a mischievous glance, got back in, and carefully drove through the gates and onto the grounds of her father's sprawling estate.

At first there was just more forest; then they emerged onto grassy slopes and came out onto a lovely cleared landscape. A large old-fashioned pre-Civil War mansion stood on a slight rise dominating the scene. There were several figures seated around its large porch, and at sight of the red sports car some of them waved.

Beyond and around the grounds Mike noticed a number of other structures, very modern one-story structures that could be—and as he learned were—laboratories, training halls, and workshops. Not too far away gleamed the blue waters of a lake, one of the many that dotted this central Floridian landscape—the lake Vivian had mentioned already, Skyhook's own private one.

"Swimming anyway," said Johnny. "All work and no play will make an astronaut sicken away."

As they drove up and parked before the porch of the big house, they recognized several of their Quicksilver friends. One, the red-topped marine, Orin

They carefully drove onto the grounds of her father's estate.

McMahan, called out: "How was the trip? We beat you here by two hours."

Mike climbed out. "Nothing to talk about," he said, looking around for a certain face and finding it missing. "Has Rod arrived yet?"

"Him?" said Orin. "He's the last. Telephoned from Washington an hour ago. Said he failed to make a good connection and will be arriving later this afternoon as a result. Didn't know you worried so much about him. He doesn't seem to worry about you."

"Oh, he just loves us all in his own clever way," sang out Johnny, adding in a voice low enough for only Mike to hear, "like a fox."

CHAPTER 7

SKYHOOK

SKYHOOK was a wonderful place. During the next few days Mike got to know and love it. It was quiet, it was restful, its workshops were new, modern, air-conditioned, and a pleasure to study in. He became familiar with the study room, where the astronauts boned up on their text work, refreshed themselves on their math and aerial geography, worked out problems in navigation, studied the latest findings from the satellites.

He got a kick out of the gym, where they worked indoors, and the big layout, where they exercised outdoors. He found the laboratory a challenge, for it was there that a full-size space capsule rested, similar to the one they had already studied at Langley, similar to the one in which each man would someday ride into space.

Each of the seven got to master the capsule and its engineering. It was cramped, but spacious enough

77

for the tasks its rider would have to do. They all learned the dials and what they would signify. They worked over the capsule with wrench and screw driver, taking it apart, examining its various delicate mechanisms, tracing its wirings, and putting it together again. Nobody knew what emergency would call for this knowledge when out in space: lives might depend on being able to get promptly to the root of any trouble.

The lake was another blessing. They swam and played waterball and did some serious skin-diving.

Ever before them were the new target dates. Hart Williams was due to go in three days, and he was taking it calmly. He joked, he studied, and he seemed indifferent. But, underneath, Mike could sense Hart's growing tension.

The Redstone rocket was not as big as the Atlas, and it was considered one of the most perfected. It had served as the first stage of several ambitious space satellite attempts, and it had been chosen for this first man-into-space effort because it was powerful enough to carry a heavy pay load and had been tested enough to be nearly safe.

But never entirely safe. The one thing every one of them knew was that no liquid-fuel rocket could ever be described as foolproof or completely safe. After twenty successful shots, the twenty-first Atlas still

Each got to master the capsule.

blew up on the pad. The Redstone was as reliable as anything based upon a wildly reacting, fizzing, sputtering, ultrafrigid frozen gas could be. It was a rocket if it worked—a murderous monster bomb if it didn't.

Nobody could predict with certainty which any particular rocket would be. The men of Project Quicksilver would have to take their chances.

There was something else they were taking chances on, and that was something they couldn't study. It was the question of their unknown enemy, the one who had tried several times to sabotage or destroy them. They didn't discuss it, but they never entirely forgot it.

The five astronauts who had not been with Mike and Johnny were never told about the attack on Mike's plane on the way to Florida. Mike had gone to Colonel Drummond as soon as he was able to break away from his friends on his arrival; and when no one could overhear, he had told the colonel what had happened.

The colonel was very grim about it. He cautioned Mike to silence, then got in touch with the intelligence agents connected with his projects. They put in a search, keeping secret their purpose. They found there were several Voodoo planes in flight-readiness at a number of fields—Air Force and National Guard

Reserve—on the day of the attack. But they could not find out which was the one that had been taken up without authority. Several persons might have taken them up, but each of the aviators apparently had a foolproof excuse. Someone had covered his tracks very cleverly, very cleverly indeed.

At one field, a man vaguely answering the description of the wanted criminal Cahoon had been seen loitering near the field—a gaunt man with a curious small scar. Strange to say, there was also a report of an unidentified young officer's having been seen near that particular field's operations building— a stocky pale-blond chap with cold gray eyes whom nobody could remember having seen before or since on that field.

It couldn't have been Rod Harger, Drummond was quite sure, because hadn't Harger come in from Washington, many miles away, and hadn't he been able to account for his time through the fact that he'd been visiting with his father? Of course—so Rod was in the clear.

Mike wondered about that, but there is a great difference between suspicion and proof. Besides, Cahoon was a good enough suspect.

One result of this, though, was that again, as had happened before during the X-15 flights, the astronauts were issued side arms—army pistols—and told

Cahoon and Rod Harger, Sr.

to keep them handy. There was a certain amount of joking about this from those who had not personally been attacked. But they followed orders.

The boys were lodged in the big house. Old though it was, the mansion had been air-conditioned and equipped with modern appliances. The rooms upstairs were large and spacious, and six of the astronauts teamed up in twos in them. Johnny and Mike shared one room. Rod Harger chose to be the odd man and he had a smaller room all to himself near the stairs.

As for Vivian, she had been brightly and noisily present for supper that first night in the big dining room of the old mansion, when all the Quicksilver bunch gathered together for the first time. Drummond and Dr. Holderlin shared the main table with Dr. Van Ness and his charming wife, but it was the chattering Vivian who held them all.

By discreet questioning, Drummond proved to himself that Vivian had in fact seen nothing of the Voodoo attacker. Which, he said afterwards to Dr. Van Ness when he told him about it, was a good thing. She'd have had a hard time keeping quiet about it to her girl friends back in school.

As it was, they had to impress her several times about the necessity for keeping mum about everything at Skyhook, especially about the astronauts. But Vivian forced a bargain.

"If I can't talk about them, you've got to promise to let me know when they get shot off. I want to go along with you, Daddy, to Canaveral and see it all."

Reluctantly, her father agreed to this. "But you can't go to the blockhouse," he said. "We'll let you get as far as the roadblock outside the Cape. You can see it plenty well from there once it's off the ground."

Had he known what was being discussed at that very moment in a room at a motel not very far away from that very roadblock station near Cape Canaveral, he would not have made even that pledge.

CHAPTER 8

THE MOONBRITE CONSPIRACY

RUNNING for hundreds of miles up and down the Atlantic Coast of the Florida peninsula is a strip of sand and soil that is separated from the actual coast of Florida by a strip of water known as the Indian River. At various points along this outer strip are fine beaches and small villages—swimming resorts devoted to happy vacationing.

At one point along the central Florida coast, opposite the city of Cocoa, this strip of oceanside beach juts out unexpectedly several miles into the sea. It forms a triangle of sand projecting beyond the coastline of the rest of the state. This is known as Cape Canaveral. The cape until a few years ago was a barren strip of desolate sand and tangled wild underbrush. Its only sign of man was a lighthouse and beacon set at the tip to warn vessels to steer clear of its shoals.

The coming of the rocket age was to change all

that. The lighthouse and its beacon still stand and are still operated. But they stand now amid a strange mushroom growth of towers, concrete mounds, slowly revolving radio antennae, and the hissing, steaming trails of rocket fuels. Cape Canaveral is

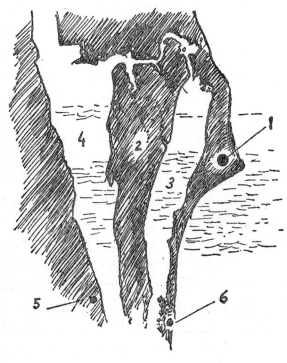

1. *Cape Canaveral*
2. *Merritt Island*
3. *Banana River*
4. *Indian River*
5. *Cocoa*
6. *Cocoa Beach*

now officially known as the Air Force Missile Test Center. Privately it has been called Earthstrip One, or Spaceport, U.S.A. It is the first and main launching station for rockets into outer space in the Western Hemisphere.

As this outthrust of sand comes in on its southern side it rejoins the main beach—a sandy strip which in this part of Florida has between it and the mainland a large island known as Merritt Island and, therefore, two rivers to cross, the outer one known as the Banana River, the inner one still the Indian.

Down a few miles from the missile base lies the resort of Cocoa Beach. A little further south of Cocoa Beach is Patrick Air Force Base, which is officially charged with the duty of supervising and managing the operations at Canaveral. The area between Patrick's neatly laid out military buildings and the outer guard posts of the cape has become a boom town for the space age. Here have sprung up housing for the men who work at the rocket pads and brand new motels for visiting engineers, guests, and those staying at the space works for brief tasks.

At one such motel, a beautiful place whose swimming pool that afternoon resounded with the shouts of boys and girls splashing and swimming—the sons and daughters of the missilemen—a small car with local license plates drew up and a man got out.

He was a short, slender, nervous man in his middle thirties. His youngish face was already lined with the strain of many hours spent in close proximity to danger. He was a missileman, one of the thousands working at Canaveral, but today, which was to have been one of his days off, he had a strange appointment.

He glanced at a telephone memo note in his hand, checked the room number, and then walked quickly down the line of doors that marked the lodging quarters of the Moonbrite Motel and found the one he sought. Hesitantly, he knocked.

The door opened and the man who stood inside said, "Hello, Jethro, come on in. It's been a long time since I saw you last."

Jethro Manson entered the room, studying his host. In spite of the warm welcome, he really didn't know Captain Tench too well. He had seen him last several years ago, when his host was an Air Force officer and was engaged in some rather unsavory activities.

Manson looked at Tench carefully as he sat down and was offered a cigarette. He started to reach for one, then shook his head.

Manson squirmed in his seat. There was something about this he didn't like, hadn't liked from the start. He'd come only because of a phone call from

Tench, who had mentioned a certain nasty episode involving the sale of stolen army supplies and equipment that Manson had been mixed up in years ago. At that time Manson had been in the service and located on the same base along the border with Tench. They had been able to get away with their unauthorized use of planes for their criminal flights into Mexico to meet their buyers, Tench doing the piloting, Manson managing the task of getting the stolen goods on and off the plane. He had quit this illegal traffic before it was too late, and during his security check for his present position it hadn't come to light.

Of course, Manson reflected, Tench could hardly expose him without exposing himself. But he wanted to cut this meeting short as rapidly as possible.

"I don't have much time, Captain," he said. "Shall we get down to business? What can I do for you?"

The man he had known as Tench—a man known to others as Cahoon—merely smiled at him. "I guess we can do a lot for each other," he said. "I understand that you are the Pad Control Officer for the Redstone operation."

Manson nodded. "That's right. Of course, we don't fire only Redstones, but when we do, they go from our pad."

"It's a good job," said Cahoon, "and you're to be congratulated." He reached into his pocket and took out a flat case. After opening it, he showed its contents to Manson. The missileman looked at it, and what he saw were papers that indicated the bearer to be an operative of Air Force Intelligence.

He could not know that the papers were carefully forged by underworld counterfeiters who had received a remarkably high fee for the dishonest task. But Cahoon was a man who had made many contacts with the criminal world since his dishonorable discharge from his country's service.

"As you see," he said to his visitor, "I am operating on secret orders, and I'm here in connection with the forthcoming tests of the Project Quicksilver astronauts."

This knowledge itself was of such a top-secret nature that it convinced Manson that his host was genuine. The men at the pad had been briefed on this project themselves only a few days before, and they had been warned about the highly classified nature of the work.

Manson nodded. Cahoon, silent for a while to impress his visitor more, whispered, "You are being asked by headquarters, through me, to undertake a very delicate task in connection with these coming shots."

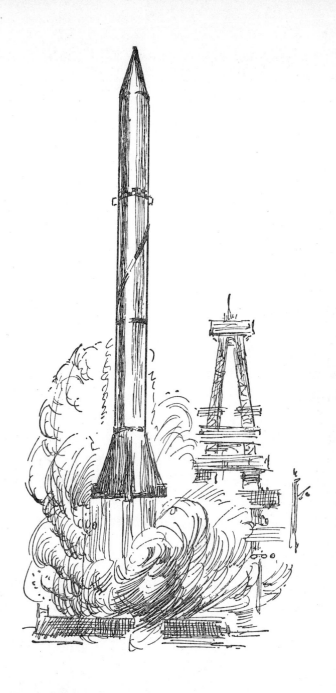

The missileman leaned forward, a little surprised, a little flattered. "Why me? What's up?"

As the Pad Control Officer he was primarily in charge of the technicians who put the rocket together, did the actual work of preparing it to go. But he was not in control of the actual launching.

Cahoon tapped his forged papers significantly. "It's desired that the first three of these Quicksilver flights not be successful. We are anxious to test the reactions of the astronauts and to test the emergency safety factors of the capsule they will ride." He paused while Manson frowned.

"You are being asked to make certain minor adjustments in the Redstones carrying the first three tests so that they will have to be destroyed either at take-off or shortly afterwards. These—uh—alterations are such as are not to be discoverable during the countdown and checkoff. Only you can do it."

Manson paled. "But why?" he said. "That's sabotage. That destroys an awful lot of work—and, besides, doesn't it put the lives of the astronauts in danger?"

Cahoon's lips drew down in a thin, tight line. "Yes, but that's exactly what we want. These capsules are designed for maximum protection. We intend that the first three Redstone shoots be merely for the purpose of testing these safety measures. The first real shoot intended to go the whole way is to be the fourth.

"Now it won't do if this fact is known. Naturally, it must be secret, and each time it must come as an emergency to all hands. Therefore, I am ordering you, on behalf of my superiors, to make these flights abortive."

Manson sat back, puzzled. This ran against all the things he had ever seen or heard of at Canaveral. It was incredible. Yet Cahoon had the credentials, knew of the top-secret shoots, and it sounded authentic.

"How can I go about sabotaging such flights?" asked Manson slowly.

"That's up to you," said Cahoon. "There's hundreds and thousands of things on a liquid-fuel rocket that can go wrong. Just a bolt loosened at the last minute, a tiny wire disconnected, a line clogged, anything. You're one of the last to leave the pad. It shouldn't be difficult for you to make a little twist or drop a little screw in such a way that it'll never be detected until the blastoff."

He leaned back. "Besides," he said, "this is official. After all," he went on casually, looking at the ceiling, "we've done a few things together in the past that weren't exactly ethical. So why should you worry, when now it's to be done as part of the secret plans?"

Manson recognized the hint of blackmail when he heard it. He had a wife and two young children now, living in a new home at Cocoa Beach. He couldn't afford to have something ruin his job now. If this was official, it was all right. But . . . well, even if it wasn't, how could they trace it to him? So many things could go wrong on a rocket, even without trying.

"Only the first three tests," he said. "There are to be seven flights, one a week."

Cahoon nodded. "Just the first three. The fourth is to come off all right. In fact, make sure it does."

Manson sat back. His hand was shaking a little, and he felt himself perspiring, though the room was air-conditioned. "I think I'll have a cigarette after all," he said. Maybe, he thought, it might quiet his nerves.

Cahoon smiled and exhaled softly as he offered the pack to his visitor.

CHAPTER 9

REDSTONE BLASTOFF

THE REDSTONE missile stood gleaming-white on its pad, and around its base swirled clouds of mist. Even as it stood, within a short time of its moment of launching, liquid oxygen was being fed into its great tanks, and this process would continue right up to five minutes before launching.

Liquid oxygen—or LOX, as it is called by the missilemen—is so cold that in ordinary temperatures it boils furiously away. Since alcohol and LOX are the main fuels of the huge rocket, in order to keep the tanks full, pumping has to continue right up to the critical moment.

So the big rocket stood there, veiled in clouds of white fumes, as the afternoon sun shed its hot rays down over the scene at the pad at Canaveral. It stood there, a round strange tower sixty-three feet high, tall and thin, painted white, and at the moment held down by the red framework of a skeleton structure of metal beams that was the movable gantry. This gantry, a structure over nine stories high, still held the forms of white-helmeted men clustered around its upper portion.

At the top of the rocket, instead of the pointed nose cone that is usually associated with such missiles, there was a glistening metallic bump painted a bright orange. It was something like a top, not too big, but with a long projecting stem of its own on top. This was the capsule. There was still a half hour to go before launching. At that moment a slim figure came rising up on the open-framework elevator that formed part of the gantry. He was dressed in a metallic coverall and his head was concealed by a deep helmet. Through the transparent front could be seen the good-looking features of Hart Williams, his dark eyes twinkling beneath the wide white helmet of the Air Force jet flier. Rising on the elevator along with him was the bearded figure of Dr. Van Ness.

The two stepped out at the top and found themselves on a level with the capsule, sitting in its niche astride the fuming Redstone. Dr. Van Ness said a word or two to the spacesuited astronaut, and then two of the helmeted technicians helped Williams climb into the tiny, narrow hatch of the capsule. When he had disappeared from view, they let the hatch close and stepped back. One of these men,

Williams climbed into the tiny hatch.

the Pad Control Officer, could be seen to be mopping his brow as he stepped back. It was a hot day, but that was not the reason.

However, if Manson was nervous, he was not the only one. Everyone at the pad was in high tension. This might well be an historic moment. If the flight went off as scheduled, it might go down in history as the very beginning of the ladder to the moon. There had been the X-15, but that was essentially a laboratory rocket. These huge ballistic missiles, the direct descendants of the V-2, were the real space-travel rockets.

From the viewpoint of rocketry, the Redstone is already old-fashioned, if you consider that liquid-fuel rockets really do not go back beyond 1943. It was a descendant of that first German cargo rocket which was built by a madman to revenge himself by senseless slaughter of innocent civilians of London after it had been obvious that Germany had lost the war.

But the men who had built the V-2, under orders, had not had insane slaughter as their objective. They had been men who dreamed of space-flight, and when the war was over they had come to the United States and had worked there for their adopted country to put the knowledge of rocketry to the service of humanity. The Redstone had been developed by this original team of engineers. It was named after the famous Redstone Arsenal at Huntsville, Alabama, where this first pioneering work had been accomplished.

The Redstone was already a mass-produced rocket, and since 1958 it had been part of the defense arsenal of America. There were teams of Army men trained to handle the Redstone and field detachments were already in operation along the frontiers of the free world's security lines.

Here at Canaveral, the Army would ordinarily have handled the Redstone, too, but this NASA-directed flight was special. The pad was one of the line facing the Atlantic, side by side with the Atlas and the Thor launching setups, from which the Explorer and Midas satellites had been launched.

The time was rapidly nearing for this first shoot. Dr. Van Ness made his way down, followed by all the other men in the white helmets, save two, one of whom was Manson.

Van Ness went to the blockhouse and entered its thick-walled mound. Inside he stood to the rear, away from the busy engineers who were completing the countdown. Colonel Drummond and two astronauts, Stacey and McMahan, were already there. They watched the flickering television screens at the front of the blockhouse with concentration. It is dangerous to be so close to a rocket when it is firing, and from inside a blockhouse there are only two means of visual observation. One is a set of four TV screens on closed channels which show a view of the rocket from four sides. The other is a group of periscopes whose eyes project through the fifteen-foot-thick wall of the concrete mound and allow a direct view of the fumes and the frame.

Stacey and McMahan were in the blockhouse because they were next on the list. Out at sea, very near to Grand Bahama Island, about one hundred and fifty miles away from Canaveral, was a white-painted naval vessel. Aboard it were Dr. Holderlin and two more astronauts, Rod Harger and Jack Lannigan. If all went well, the capsule would come down somewhere nearby. They were to observe its return to Earth, assist in the recovery of the capsule and the questioning of Hart Williams.

On a wooden platform about five thousand feet away from the Redstone pad stood two more astronauts and a small group of engineers and observers. Mike Mars and Johnny Bluehawk held powerful binoculars in their hands and were watching the fuming rocket anxiously through them.

From a loud-speaker set up on one side of the observation platform they could hear the calm droning of the countdown going on. This stand, which

Mike and Johnny were watching the fuming rocket.

was built for the use of newspapermen and magazine writers who covered the big events at Canaveral, was equipped for listening in on the blockhouse events. It was sufficiently far away from the actual pad to be out of danger in the event of explosion or disaster.

At the moment there were no reporters around: it was intended that there should not be. The only outsiders who could tell that something was doing were far away on the highway that passes Canaveral on the other side of the Banana River. Doubtless there were cars parked there with tourists wondering if they would see something flash into the sky and would catch a glimpse of something wonderful. But what they would see, if they saw anything, would not now be explained by the Air Force.

Mike Mars watched the thin lines of vapor curl around the gleaming rocket. "Five minutes to go," he said, echoing the voice that came to him from the blockhouse.

Johnny, standing by his side, was silent. He was thinking of what it must be like to be Hart Williams, resting silently in his cushioned, form-fitting seat inside the narrow confines of the metal cylinder. In a few minutes he would be thrust back by the terrific acceleration of the powerful rockets; then he would be forced upwards, rising atop a cloud of blazing, burning gases. Again he would be freed of his weight as the rocket burned out. His capsule would then disconnect from the empty shell and he would come down to earth from the airless realm of outer space, riding on his retro-rockets and then on his parachute.

Each of them lived in his mind the moments of the Redstone ride. They had all trained for it; they had spent hours inside the capsule, learning every trick of it. They knew it, and yet it was a moment of great excitement now that one of them was at last testing out in practice what they had played out so often at Skyhook and, before that, at Langley.

Mike spoke softly. "They're taking the gantry away. It's sliding back. Three minutes now."

His gray eyes stared through his glasses at the slim figure, standing like a fairy tower by itself amid the greenery of the sandy stretches. He could see the protuberance of the capsule atop the tower. The fumes had ceased coming, for no longer were the fuel pumps connected.

"Two minutes," said the countdown voice. Beside Mike, Johnny was watching the white rocket, too, and now all the others on the platform raised their binoculars and focused them on the Redstone, where a human being was waiting to rise into space.

"He's a cool boy, Hart is," said Mike quietly. "He didn't seem at all worried at breakfast this morning."

"Why should he?" said Johnny. "He's an astronaut, isn't he? Haven't you always said that knowledge is power? And hadn't he been given the knowledge of what he is doing?"

"That's right," said Mike. "To be an astronaut is a proud thing, but it all depends on knowing exactly what you're doing every second."

"Thirty seconds," said Johnny. "Hart knows what he's doing. So would you. Here goes."

"Twenty seconds," said the countdown voice, and they all drew in their breath. In sudden silence, everyone on the observation platform watched the distant figure of the silent white rocket.

In the blockhouse, the same silence prevailed, save for the quiet voices of the men responding to their instruments.

At the roadblock a group of three from Skyhook stood beside a little red car and watched in silence.

Along the highway, standing among the chatting rubberneck tourists, Cahoon, raised his field glasses and tried to see what he could.

CHAPTER 10

EMERGENCY FLIGHT

"THREE, two, one, zero," intoned the voice over the late afternoon air. Mike Mars held his field glasses tightly to his eyes and watched.

For a moment it seemed as if nothing was happening. The white rocket stood there quietly. Then it could be seen that vapor was hissing down and wisping around its base. There was a cloud of grayish-white steam suddenly billowing about and the faint suggestion of red, as if fire were somewhere beneath that steam.

Mike knew that water was pouring along the base of the rocket, flooding it as the engines were beginning to pour their flaming gases below. The water was there to keep the pad and the exposed tail fins cool against the terrific heat of the burning gases.

Still the rocket seemed to stand there in its growing cloud of gases, as if unable to move. Then it began at last to rise, but slowly, incredibly slowly. It seemed to hang above the ground, poised on a raging cloud of steam and vapor and fire, one foot, a foot and a half, two feet.

One almost expected this tower, hanging so strangely above the ground, to topple over—but it didn't. Instead, it began to rise higher and higher, and as it rose it gradually, visibly increased speed.

Mike moved his lips soundlessly. "Go it," he tried to whisper, "go on, go on." But his lips were dry and he could say nothing.

The white Redstone rocket rose still more. Now it was half its length above the ground, and the ground was covered with a small lake of vapors like the spray from an ocean. It rose again, began to move fast. Up and up, and then . . .

"It's twisting!" cried Mike. "It's twisting!" And the white rocket was turning, wavering, beginning to shake and twist around.

"Eject!" whispered Johnny next to him.

"Get out!" called someone else. "Break loose," came unconsciously from Stacey's lips in the blockhouse. Dr. Van Ness merely stood in the back, eyes glued to the television screen, face pale.

There was no need to give orders. Hart Williams was trained. The rocket itself had automatic equipment on it which would sense when something was going wrong. The equipment acted. If it hadn't, Hart would have acted himself a split second later.

At the observation post, Mike saw it happen. The Redstone's white glistening length was two hundred feet in the air and already twisting on its fiery tail. There was a puff of fire at its nose, and suddenly the little orange bulb at the top parted from the rocket and went up on its own fiery power.

The little capsule shot away from the white rocket, and its escape rockets blasted it on, upwards, away from the path of the wild Redstone. Mike followed it with his glasses and saw it go on into the blue sky, saw the fire of its escape rockets vanish, saw the capsule soar on, a tiny dot that seemed to swing over to one side near the ocean, to be over the water, and then he saw a red-and-white-striped mass pop out of it and turn at once into a parachute.

The capsule began to come down now, a half mile away, over the water. Mike turned his glasses from it to the rocket. The Redstone was wriggling erratically several hundred feet up now, beginning to turn, and, even as he watched, there came an explosion. The white slender tube seemed to break apart in the middle, shattered by black smoke and arched over. There was another explosion, and then the smoking mass plunged down far into the sea beyond the cape.

There was an emergency officer at the cape whose duty it was to destroy while in the air any rocket that was going astray. After the capsule had made its escape, this officer had pressed the "destruct" button and the mechanisms within the Redstone had torn it apart.

This Mike knew, and this is what had happened.

He and Johnny turned and dashed down the wooden stairs of the observation platform. They jumped into the car that awaited them and tore across the roads to the Redstone pad. As they arrived, Van Ness and the others were coming out.

"It's all right," called the bearded scientist as he saw the two boys. "We got word Williams came down in the sea safely and made good his escape. A Navy boat is picking him up."

"But—what happened?" asked Mike. "What went wrong?"

Van Ness shrugged. "They're studying the tapes. It looks like something jammed in the guidance mechanism. Maybe just something slight like a loose screw. It doesn't take much to do it."

"Gosh, that's terrible," said Mike. "What a bad break for Hart."

Van Ness looked back at the pad, which was still smoking from the launching. "We've got to expect

The rocket exploded in a cloud of black smoke.

a certain amount of errors. Human beings are not perfect, you know, and what we do cannot always be perfect either."

"Besides, we've still got Joe Stacey," said Johnny. "Maybe the Navy will do the honors after all."

Stacey, who was standing beside Van Ness, smiled. "You can rely on the Navy to come through."

The others laughed, and it broke the uneasiness. The bearded scientist went over and joined Colonel Drummond in a staff car. "We're going over to pick up Hart and talk to him. The rest of you fellows can go and eat supper. Meet me back at Patrick tonight and we'll return to Skyhook."

The four astronauts went back to the car and climbed in. "Where to?" said Mike at the wheel.

"There's a good place to eat in Cocoa Beach," said McMahan. "Let's go there and we can talk this thing out over some good sea food."

Mike nodded, and the car turned and went away. The four drove in silence—each man still a little bemused by the sudden disaster and a little sobered from the shock and disappointment—past the guard post, down the main road, and on the road that ran along the highway.

Mike spotted a little red sports car proceeding up the road ahead of them and he deliberately slowed down to let it get away. He had a good idea who was in it, and this night he didn't want a flood of girlish chatter to interrupt his thoughts.

Going slowly as he did, he passed the sign of the Moonbrite Motel. A car was pulling in there. Out of the corner of his eye, he saw a man rising to get out of it. He didn't see him clearly, for he was driving, but he saw him enough.

A familiar something about that man. Mike turned his head and looked back. The man was going around a corner, and he couldn't make him out.

Mike looked back at the road. He sure felt hungry. He drove on a little bit. Who was that man? His mind nagged at him.

Then, as he approached the one-block-long business section of Cocoa Beach, it struck him. He braked the car violently.

"Hey!" yelled his passengers, shaken forward by the jolt. "What are you trying to do?"

Mike twisted the wheel, turned the car sharply. Cars coming the other way pulled violently to a halt at the unexpected interruption. Johnny clutched at Mike's arm. "What's up?" he cried.

Mike completed reversing the car. "That was Cahoon!" he said. "I spotted him. At the Moonbrite!"

The car charged back toward the motel, with four suddenly aroused astronauts straining forward like hawks who have sighted their prey.

CHAPTER 11

KEEP YOUR EYES OPEN!

MIKE brought the car into the parking space in front
of the Moonbrite Motel with a fast jolting stop that
would have thrown his passengers from their seats
had they not already been straining to jump. As the
car stopped, Mike leaped out of the door.

Already Mike noticed that the car he had seen was
no longer there. He dashed into the office while the

three others split and ran down the line of rooms that made up the motel.

At the desk Mike banged for the manager, and in a moment that individual came out. Hastily Mike described Cahoon. "Have you a man who looks like that registered here? He called himself Cahoon. Or maybe Tench?"

Mike knew the real name of his prey, for he had heard it after Air Intelligence had identified the man who had caused the near disaster in the X-15 trials.

The manager shook his head. "We've nobody by either of those names listed. I don't recall anyone answering that description, but . . . just a minute." He went back and in a moment returned with a young lady. "She handles the desk when I'm not here; perhaps she knows him."

Mike repeated the description, trying to keep calm, though he knew that the man might be escaping even as he talked. The girl listened, thought a moment. "I wonder if that couldn't be Mr. Smith," she said at last. "He's in Room 14 and he had a scar such as you describe."

Mike thanked her and ran out. He saw the others coming back from their quick survey of the grounds. He called to them and the four ran to the room on the ground level with the number 14.

Mike knocked, but there was no answer. He tried

the door, but it was locked. As he knocked again, the manager came up. Quickly Mike explained their urgency. He couldn't tell him too much, but he made it plain that they had to know where Smith was. The manager was finally persuaded to use his master key on the door. He threw it open.

The room was empty. There was evidence of a hasty departure—one of great haste indeed, for apparently "Smith" had merely grabbed his bags, thrown in what he could get his hands on, and run for his car.

They found pajamas, a comb, a pair of slippers. They looked into the desk and the wastebasket. There were some crumpled sheets in it, but nothing of consequence. The manager was upset, however. "He still owed me for today's rent," he complained.

"Well, when we find him, you can get it out of him. It'll be the least of his problems." Mike said.

"What are we waiting for?" put in Johnny Bluehawk. "He must be driving away right now and he can't be too far."

"That's right!" yelled someone else, and the four astronauts piled out the room and ran to their car. Jumping in pell-mell, Mike turned the auto and chased away in the direction opposite the beach village.

But though they raced crazily along the road all

the way across the causeway that connects Cocoa Beach with Merritt Island and then with the city of Cocoa, crossing the Banana River and the Indian River, they did not see the car with Cahoon. It had been too late.

They returned to Skyhook after a night session at Patrick in which Hart Williams, a little shaken up but still smiling gamely, had joined them at NASA headquarters and described his experiences in detail.

He described them again the next day, back at Skyhook. This time, at a morning session in one of the study buildings on the pleasant but guarded estate, they were able to thrash out the mishap in detail.

Van Ness and Drummond were not downhearted about the failure of the Redstone the first time. "This one bad break should just about guarantee the success of the next flight," said the scientist. "According to the records and the engineers' observations, it must have been something as simple as a misplaced screw in one part of the directional apparatus.

"Actually," Dr. Van Ness went on, "it was a very successful flight in one important respect. It showed that the capsule's safety mechanism is functioning just as planned. In spite of the sudden eject and the short height from the ground at which it occurred, Williams came down unhurt and was able to make his escape without special difficulty."

Hart Williams ran a hand through his crew-cut black hair. "I will say that nothing is ever going to overcome the surprise, though. I knew the capsule was safe, but even so, when you're all keyed up over going into outer space, the sudden disaster sure comes as a shock. They'll never figure a way to keep the man inside from being scared stiff for the first second. Just like having someone suddenly yell in your ear when you least expect it. Just can't help yourself—you got to jump. And, brother, I jumped!"

"It's Joe's turn to get the bounce next," laughed Mike. "Think it'll holler at you?" Mike looked at the slender Navy pilot, Joe Stacey.

Stacey grinned. "Not me. Hart's had the Old Maid in this game. I expect to get my fast trip to the Bahamas in good style."

Later that day Mike and Johnny Bluehawk were called aside by the colonel. "Now, are you really sure that man you saw was Cahoon?" Drummond asked them.

Mike nodded. "I only saw him out of the corner of my eye, but I'm sure it was him."

"Besides," said Johnny, "the way he cleared out in such a hurry was further proof. The girl at the motel said he answered the description, too."

Colonel Drummond looked worried. "I have notified our intelligence investigators and they should even now be over at the Moonbrite checking the room for fingerprints. We'll keep a check around as best we can without alerting too many law forces. Frankly, I think it was Cahoon, but I can't figure what he's up to around here."

"Whatever it is, it's no good," said Mike. "Can we do a little looking around, too?"

The colonel shook his head. "You boys have got to keep up your training. Let the men whose business it is to find criminals do their job. Your business happens to be outer space. Right?"

"Sure thing," said Mike and Johnny together.

Nonetheless, the two did not allow the matter to get entirely out of their minds. Skyhook was a place for study and for relaxation but, underneath, the two young fellows felt the tension rising.

One Redstone shoot had failed. Could it have been sabotage? Mike discussed this at some length with Johnny and the two could not agree on any answer. "I'd say we'll have to see what happens next time," said Johnny slowly. "I don't see how Cahoon could have got at the rocket. Every man at the pad is the same as was there for months past. They're all tried and true."

"Nothing is perfect," said Mike. "We'll have to keep our eyes open."

CHAPTER 12

GO ON, JOE!

ONCE AGAIN a gleaming Redstone rocket waited on its pad for the final countdown that would send it hurtling into space with its human load. This time it was the slender form of Joseph Stacey that climbed into the capsule perched on top of the nose.

Joe hadn't been nervous, at least not that anyone could see, but Mike had noticed that this time there was a good deal less bantering during the last few hours. He and the others present at the cape for the shooting had taken a light lunch with Joe at one of the food trucks that Pan American Aviation sent around the various rocket pads at midday.

The "gaggin' wagon," as missilemen called the lunch truck, was parked just outside the blockhouse, and five astronauts were devouring sandwiches, milk, and coffee during the break. The others present besides Joe were Mike and Johnny, Hart Williams and

Orin McMahan. As before, Rod and Jack Lannigan were out at sea.

They kidded around as usual, but the jokes were met with a certain forced laughter. The mishap of the week before had brought home to all of them in a way no lectures or demonstrations could have done just how dangerous this Quicksilver Project could be.

There were several of the men from the gantry clustering around, too, having a quick bite, and among them was one who had been briefly introduced to Mike and the rest. This one, the Pad Control Officer, Jethro Manson, had simply nodded rather offhandedly and made a rapid return to the rocket, standing upright in its frame. Mike paid no attention to Manson's apparent unwillingness to be friendly, for the other missilemen's interest more than made up for it. Besides, Mike knew that Manson's duties called for responsibility and that time was pressing.

Now, as Mike stood again at the observation platform listening to the final words of the countdown, he kept his glasses glued to the Redstone. He put out of his mind his concern about Cahoon and concentrated on the rocket. Next to him, Johnny stood in silence also.

Once more the countdown worked its way to the zero moment. Once again the clouds of steam swirled around the base of the straining rocket as the first fiery gases began to bellow forth from the tubes. Again the roar and rising howl of the rocket's engines began to rage across the entire cape.

The rocket lifted slowly, the gleaming capsule on its nose rising with it toward the afternoon sky. Mike watched tensely, and as he watched he felt himself whispering, "Go on, go on! Up, boy, up!"

Johnny, next to him, was whispering the same thing, and as they watched the rocket struggling upward slowly on its lengthening pillar of fire they called out louder, as if cheering a runner rounding base: "Go on! Get up there, Joe!"

The rocket rose smoothly, and as it moved it went faster and faster. It cleared the gantry length, it began to accelerate, and, as they watched, its speed grew.

"It's going!" Johnny called, elated. It was . . . it was. It was up there, now a hundred feet, now two hundred feet, now three, four, more. Rising steadily, swiftly, beautifully.

Up and up it went, now a thousand feet, now more and more. Two thousand feet, and running smoothly, a white-yellow jet of fire burning brilliantly from its tail, a white pencil rising in the blue sky.

"Turn, fellow, turn now. Out over the ocean, boy," whispered Mike now, lowering his voice in a strained fashion. It was high enough, the automatic gyroscopic controls should now be turning the rocket, should now be directing it on a course out over the ocean, rising high into the stratosphere on an arc that would end in an island rendezvous far away.

But it was not turning. It was continuing straight up, higher and higher. "What's wrong with the controls?" whispered Mike in a shocked voice. "It's not going right. It's not turning."

Johnny, beside him, had stopped breathing, was simply staring through binoculars with strained face and pinched lips.

Mike watched now in silence, feeling suddenly sick. "They'll have to stop it," he said, and even as he spoke the moment that they all dreaded had come.

There was a tiny puff of smoke from the nose, and the capsule suddenly broke away, whirled around on a tiny rocket arc of its own, high, high up in the sky. A few seconds afterward the Redstone abruptly crumpled, flew apart in a blast of black smoke.

"It's been destroyed," said Mike, lowering his glasses. "The gyro controls failed. Joe's coming down."

Johnny let go his breath, which he had been holding. "There's the parachute now," he said, pointing.

Mike looked in the direction of the young Cheyenne's finger, then focused his field glasses. He found

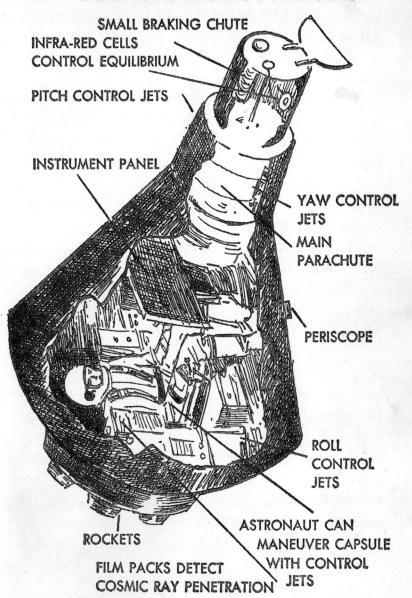

SPOILER TURNS CAPSULE IF YAW JETS FAIL

SMALL BRAKING CHUTE

INFRA-RED CELLS
CONTROL EQUILIBRIUM

PITCH CONTROL JETS

INSTRUMENT PANEL

YAW CONTROL
JETS

MAIN
PARACHUTE

PERISCOPE

ROLL
CONTROL
JETS

ROCKETS

ASTRONAUT CAN
MANEUVER CAPSULE
WITH CONTROL
JETS

FILM PACKS DETECT
COSMIC RAY PENETRATION

Inside a capsule

it at last, a tiny puff of orange and white and a gleaming dot, still high in the sky but falling gently now, a mile or so out over the ocean.

"And that's the second shoot," he said. "A different trouble, anyway."

The two lowered their glasses, looked at each other silently. Then Mike suddenly clicked his tongue. "If Tench—I mean Cahoon—is around, he'll be watching this. It might be a good time to look for him. I want to catch him if I can."

Johnny nodded. "Let's go. We'll make the rounds of the highway and the roadblocks."

They ran down the steps of the observation platform, found the car that had been assigned for their use, leaped in, and, with Johnny at the wheel, turned and drove fast out of the cape, past the outer guard post.

There were observers clustered around the roadblock near the post. There were tourists parked along the highways that had a view of the cape. These people were still there, excitedly discussing what they had seen.

They did not know what kind of rocket had been fired, they did not know that there had been a capsule with a human being in it, they did not know the outcome or the purpose of the firing. But somehow the fact that there was to be a firing had gotten around as it always does, and there are people who always come to watch.

There is nothing like the blasting off of a big rocket, nothing like the roaring, powerful sound of mighty engines going off. The thrill is there, even when the details of the shoot are secret.

So there were hundreds of people around on the roads, and their cars were parked up and down the beaches and highways.

Mike and Johnny drove around observing not the sky and the horizon but the people. They knew they couldn't cover the entire area, but they hoped that for once luck would be with them and they might find their man.

They had been right in the belief that Cahoon himself could not have stayed away. Cahoon was fascinated by the rockets, as much as any of the observers, and he had a personal stake as well.

Cahoon was there, but Mike and his friend never saw him. He saw their car coming up the beach road before they saw him, and he simply walked around his car, keeping himself hidden from their view.

When they were gone, he climbed into his car and drove away in the other direction. He was smiling to himself. Manson had again come through as directed. One more to go and his job would be done.

CHAPTER 13

MIAMI MONKEY BUSINESS

IN A ROOM at one of the large luxury hotels that line Miami Beach a hundred and ninety miles to the south of Cape Canaveral two men sat talking. Rod Harger, Jr., was one of them; the other seemed like an older version of the same. This was Rod's father, and he had arranged this Sunday meeting with his son to determine how their plans were going.

That Sunday, a couple of days after the second disastrous Redstone shoot, was not a study day for the astronauts. In spite of the pressing plans for the new future, the directors of Project Quicksilver knew that rest and a day of fun are also important in keeping spirits and bodies in good top trim.

Rod had been invited to join three of the astronauts in a four-handed tennis match that afternoon, but he had declined. He had also had the opportunity of joining in a day's fishing with several of the technicians. But he had announced his intention of visiting the famous resort city of Miami on Sunday, had made his leave early, and had flown down by plane from Orlando. His real business had been to meet his father. The senior Harger was not very satisfied. "I'm getting fed up with this waiting, Rod. I've spent a lot of money hiring Cahoon and his thugs and so far I've not managed to get anything back for it."

Rod shook his head. "You've got to keep on being patient," he said. "This program cannot be hurried any more than it is. Cahoon is doing very well this time. He didn't do too badly when he managed to get rid of some of the better candidates during the first examinations for astronauts. He almost succeeded with the X-15—after all, he's really very slick. And he's certainly managed to do very well now. I don't know myself how he is getting through to the Redstone pad to sabotage it, but somehow he did find a way."

The scowling face of his father did not break. "I know. Cahoon is one of the best men in his business —a born scoundrel with lots of connections. I'm paying him a good deal, believe me, and that Mike Mars fellow has given him a special personal reason, too. But we've got to get some results this time."

Rod nodded. "Well, Mike is on to Cahoon's presence, I'm sure. I've heard how Mike and his pal Johnny go prowling around after each shot. I'm sure he's suspicious. If I'd had a little better plane that time, I could have shot him down for sure. But all I could get my hands on that day we flew down here was a slower one, the Voodoo."

His father allowed a brief smile to flicker over his face. "I'm proud of you anyway. It was a good try. I know you've got it in you. You'll be going up on the fourth Redstone try. This one is going to be a good one. No tampering; it ought to go all right. That'll put you as the first man into space on a rocket. Now I've decided that when that happens we're going to see that the story leaks out to the newspapers. I don't want to wait any longer to begin to cash in on the fame and stories that will come out of it.

"I've arranged for certain newsmen to be on Grand Bahama Island at the right time—cameramen, too. If they get your story, all the efforts of the Air Force to keep the thing secret will do no good. It'll leak out. It'll make you a hero, and the NASA people will have to own up to it."

Rod nodded slowly. "I guess they can't stop you from leaking it out. There must be dozens of people at Canaveral who suspect what's going on. They're trained to secrecy but, you know, somebody can always be persuaded to talk."

"Exactly," said his father. "And when the news is out, your directors can't dare deny you the first

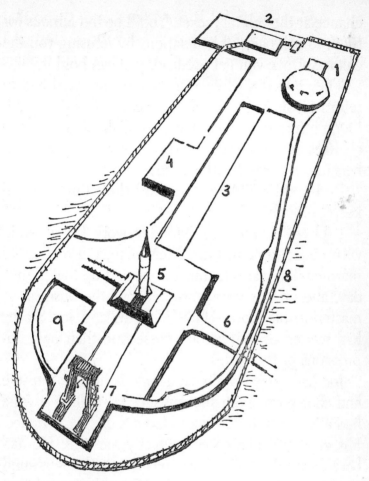

Typical missile launch site

1. Blockhouse
2. Ready room
3. Water main
4. and 9. Fuel storage
5. Ramp and test stand area
6. Drainage
7. Service tower
8. Security fence
9. (see #4)

chance at the orbital rocket. You'll be too famous for them to risk bad public relations by refusing you the chance. Once you get the lead, you can hold it."

They talked a while longer, and then Rod had to return to Skyhook. As he took leave, his father said, "Don't forget to advise me or Cahoon as to any changes in plans or dates. You have the special numbers to call to reach either of us."

Rod nodded. "After this third shot, I'm next. I'll keep in touch."

Back at Skyhook on Monday work began again with concentration. Orin McMahan, the redheaded marine pilot, was scheduled to be sent up that Thursday, and he was grimly attending to the business of mastering his work. Hart Williams and Joe Stacey had related to him second by second their own impressions of their trips.

Joe had gone up almost a mile before his capsule had shot away from the misdirected rocket, and he had a lot more to tell than Hart's shorter experience. His capsule had worked perfectly, he said. He had been in steady radio communication with the ground at all times, he had been advised from the instant that the gyro controls failed to function, he himself had made the decision to cut the capsule loose and have the rocket destroyed.

"It was smooth," Joe said, "because I was ready

for it. The whole thing went off just as if it was a mock-up in our laboratory. I zoomed up, the parachute opened, the retro-rockets slowed me down, I came down smooth as a feather, hit the water exactly as the dummy experiments had, and got myself out just like we'd been drilled.

"I was wondering only whether the boats would be there on time to pick me up. This Florida water's warm, but I still don't like floating around in it too long. They say there are sharks around sometimes."

The other astronauts were also there, and there was laughter at this. Actually, in their spacesuits, they were quite safe from the beasts of the sea— although a shark might perhaps prove a nasty customer just the same.

"I guess I was in the water fifteen minutes before they got to me. It really was a picnic." He grinned and looked at Orin. "So now it's up to you to get up there and say hello to the stars in the daytime."

Orin nodded. "Twice ought to be enough for trouble. I aim to see that it doesn't go wrong for me."

The days went on. Again a Redstone rocket was readied at Canaveral. Once more a gleaming capsule was hoisted to its nose, attached carefully, and the connections checked and rechecked.

"This time," said Dr. Van Ness, "we will shuffle the positions of the observing astronauts. Rod Harger and Jack Lannigan will be at the observation platform. Williams and Stacey will be on the ship, and they will leave tonight so as to be in position by tomorrow afternoon when the shot comes off. And it's Bluehawk's and Samson's turns to observe from inside the blockhouse."

Mike Mars was glad to hear this. Inside the blockhouse you couldn't directly see the rocket, but it was so much more exciting. He looked forward to that.

CHAPTER 14

THE THIRD COUNTDOWN

As ALWAYS, the morning of the capsule launching was one of great excitement and tension at Skyhook. The man whose chance it was to go up in the rocket was usually the calmest—it was the others who showed the effects of the coming test. Orin Mc-Mahan, for instance, was quite jovial this morning. The rest were jumping but trying to conceal it from the redheaded marine.

Orin, in fact, spent part of the morning playing tennis with one of the off-duty guards at the courts near the lake. Dr. Holderlin always felt that relaxing was the best preparation for the possible strains to come.

The rest of the astronauts were busy at their various preparations, going over once more, as they had twice before, the problems posed by the flight. Out at Canaveral the initial countdown was proceeding.

A countdown is not just something that occurs

immediately before the flight. Actually it may start many hours or even a day or two before the shoot signal. For what a countdown consists of is the careful checking of everything connected with the mighty rocket and its equipment. Every part is tested for working condition, every factor is studied and re-studied, until everything that men can do is done to assure success.

But a huge and highly complicated thing like a giant liquid-oxygen rocket can never be perfectly checked. There are too many things—but the missile-men do the best they can.

So at Canaveral, out at the pad, the countdown had begun hours in advance. Each of the valves and electrical instruments, each tank, feeder, and connecting linkup was being tested and checked off as in working condition. The Pad Control Officer was an important man in these proceedings—and well he knew that even a loose screw, a faint clogging of a tiny line, or a loose wire could spell disaster for the entire giant device.

As the day proceeded, the astronauts prepared for their various roles. Rod and Jack went off early, going by plane to the island where the capsule would come down, embarking on the observation ship to await the moment that McMahan's parachuting capsule would fall out of space into the warm waters of the Bahamas.

A little later the rest of them drove down to the cape. Mike and Johnny Bluehawk, along with Dr. Van Ness, crossed the guardhouse at the pad, entered the concrete-and-steel mushroom-shaped dome that was the blockhouse.

They passed through a doorway which was almost a tunnel, for the walls of the controlling blockhouse were no less than fifteen feet thick. "They can stand off a direct hit by the entire force of an exploding rocket," Johnny commented as they walked through the thick doorway.

Mike nodded. "They sure didn't take any chances," he said. "Some bang." He remembered the raging fury he had seen twice as the first two rockets had been detonated high in the air.

Inside, the two astronauts and the bearded scientist took a stand in the rear, out of the way of the men working. There were perhaps a dozen men in shirt sleeves sitting around the room at the dials of their indicators.

In the front of the room, high on the wall, were the clocks that indicated the time, the minutes passed since the countdown began, the holding periods involved, and the time to go. Four television screens flickered beneath the clocks, and the fuming white figure of the Redstone could be seen, still held in the framework of the gantry.

At the top they could see the shining bulb of the

capsule, and they could visualize in their mind's eye the recumbent form of their astronautic marine, clad in his space pressure suit, calmly suspended before his own indicators, waiting for the go signal.

A voice boomed through the blockhouse, "T minus thirty minutes and counting." This was the talker, the conductor of the countdown.

"Check capsule ready," his voice said.

From someone else, the reply, "Ready."

"Capsule communication operating," said the talker.

"Operating," came the voice of McMahan.

On they went, checking down each item of the rocket. Was the telemetry system operating? Yes. Was the acceleration meter functioning? Yes. Was the water pressure ready, in order to cool the base of the pad as the rocket flared? Yes.

"Launching pad cleared of personnel?" came the talker's voice. "Yes," said someone, and this meant that the engineers and mechanics had cleared away, that the rocket was standing alone now, no one nearer than the men safely inside the blockhouse.

"T minus fifteen minutes and counting," said the test control operator.

Mike and Johnny stood there quietly, watching and listening to the men sitting before their panels. Faces were tense, eyes were glued to their dials, waiting, watching for the slightest sign of something wrong.

Mike thought to himself that something had gone wrong twice in succession, in spite of all this checking. Could the trouble strike three times? Or was this the winner?

Ten minutes to go. The weather was reported in as good. The Range Safety Officer from the Central Control Building announced the air clear of aviation, the sea safe from passing vessels.

"'T minus two minutes and counting," came the steady, calm voice of the talker. Mike pursed his lips, and glanced at his friend. Johnny was staring at the television screens, his black eyes sharp, his face set.

"Missile power," said the talker. "Go," came the answer from one of the panel men.

Telemetry? Propulsion? Yes, yes.

"'T minus sixty seconds and counting."

"Range Ready light on," said a voice. Outside the warning signal was on.

"Final status check," said the talker. In order, everything was rapidly recounted. Mike glanced along the line of panels. He could see lights lit that had not been before; he could sense that now all was ready, that everything was clear.

"Twenty seconds," said the talker. "Capsule check."

"Ready," came the calm familiar tones of Orin McMahan, perched up there outside on top of the fuming, steaming mountain of fuel.

"T minus fifteen seconds," and Mike knew that outside the water was now pouring on the base of the Redstone ready to combat the heat of the blast.

Somewhere the hum of cameras began as automatic pictures were made of the readings and television views.

"Nine, eight, seven . . ."

Mike glanced around. Every face was tense, every man must at that moment have wondered whether this time a man would go into space, whether history was a matter of mere seconds away.

Dr. Van Ness had been stroking his beard; now his hand paused, held up as if caught in a photograph.

"Three, two, one . . ." The automatic relays had been started seconds back, no hand would press a switch, but at the time the rocket would be off on its own. In the capsule, McMahan must have been bracing himself, waiting for the first thrust beneath him.

"Zero."

Outside, the engines would be roaring, but the sound could not pierce the thick walls of the blockhouse. There was a moment of breathless silence as each eye scanned his panel of lights, as Mike and

"It never left," Van Ness said.

Johnny and Van Ness watched the sight in the television screens.

The rocket still stood, apparently motionless, but it could be seen that great clouds of steam were arising, that the brilliant glare of fire was spurting into the pad, that within split seconds the thing would rise, inch by inch, then foot by foot, and at last mile by mile.

But now it strained and thrust. And then——

The blockhouse shook. A distinct shock ran through the terribly thick walls and registered its blow in the surprise and unbelief on the faces inside.

At that moment, the television screens went black.

Outside, the four cameras standing in view of the rocket had simply ceased to exist.

Mike felt his feet shake as if a hammer had knocked on the floor. He turned in amazement to Dr. Van Ness. "I thought," he said, and paused. "I thought you couldn't feel the rocket leaving the earth."

He knew the answer even as he spoke, though he didn't want to admit it. The bearded scientist turned to him, his face pale.

"It never left," said Merlin Van Ness in a dry whisper. "It blew up on the pad."

CHAPTER 15

THE X-15 AGAIN

"WHAT happened to Orin?" Mike asked in a low voice. Dr. Van Ness didn't answer, but merely turned and pointed at one of the technicians inside the blockhouse.

The men were still at their places, still at their dials. Though they were visibly shaken, nobody had deserted his post. The talker's voice came through now, after a lapse.

"T plus fifteen seconds," the voice said. "Capsule report?"

"Capsule detached successfully at T plus three seconds. Telemetry still operating," said someone— a man at one of the electronic consoles that gave readings from the instruments within the capsule.

Mike felt himself breathe a sigh of relief. The talker spoke again. "Capsule report, please."

They waited, but there was no answer. Orin McMahan was silent.

Dr. Van Ness watched the instruments, whispered to Mike and Johnny. "The capsule was shot away automatically when the rocket blew. It's coming down now. Retro-rockets seem to be operating, judging from that dial reading, but I don't know about the parachute."

Someone was talking on a telephone. Mike could hear references to "outside the blockhouse." Again the capsule report came in. "Nearing the ground in slow fall."

It seemed like an hour before they finally left the blockhouse, but actually it was about ten minutes. When they dashed through the long doorway, after it had been cautiously opened, they stopped short. Outside there was a scene of devastation. The skeletons of the gantries, although moved far away, were torn and twisted. The entire ground was seared and black. Where the guardhouse had stood was a blasted ruin. Still-smoking masses of twisted metal lay strewn about, and tendrils of smoke wreathed themselves about the landscape.

They could hear the sirens of fire trucks and emergency cars speeding up to them. Mike gazed around and was struck as never before by the immense power hidden inside the space rockets.

The capsule came down on the ground, not in the water, about a thousand feet away. It had been

Outside there was a scene of devastation.

slowed by its retro-rockets; it had fallen part of the way under its parachute, which had not had full time to slow it. The ambulances got to the capsule just before Mike, Johnny, and Dr. Van Ness drove up in a staff car.

They pulled out Orin McMahan unconscious. He had suffered a broken shoulder blade, a broken left arm. He was also bruised in spots, but the remarkable shock-absorbing powers of the capsule had prevented any permanent damage.

It was a sober group of astronauts that gathered in the study hall building at Skyhook late the next morning. The fellows had hung around talking quietly about what had happened while Colonel Drummond and his two associates in the direction of Project Quicksilver had telephoned to headquarters in Washington and to other rocket bases.

Now Colonel Drummond looked around at the six young men. They looked back at him, and the question in their minds was whether the tests would be continued or called off?

"We have decided to go ahead with one more attempt to shoot a man into space on the Redstone," the colonel said slowly. The six felt their breaths going out in relief. "We will be using a new pad for the next shoot, and we are going right ahead.

"The odds against three successive accidents with

the Redstone were considered large. We are no longer certain that these were indeed accidents. But we hope to test our views once more, considering that each occurrence apparently was due to a different cause." He paused, looked at each of the young men in turn.

"I have, however, one piece of good news to announce. Talking with headquarters today, I learned that the X-15 is now ready for its second High Range flight. They are preparing it now for an attempt next week. They want one of you to leave this project temporarily and to go to Edwards Air Force Base in California for this flight.

"As you know, Mike Mars has already had his chance with the X-15, and he was quite successful. The next in line for this rocket plane was Rod Harger, who also happens to be next in line for the Redstone shoot, with Mike scheduled to follow him.

"In so far as Harger was the next qualified pilot for the X-15, we have decided to give him his chance there. So, Rod, you will pack what you need and fly out to California this afternoon. Mike Samson, here, will ride the capsule in seven days."

Rod Harger was stunned but hastily managed to conceal his astonishment. Mike was equally surprised, and he felt a sudden thrill run through him. He had expected that surely another would pioneer the rocket shoot instead of him, but now his chance was upon him.

The rest of that day passed like a dream. What had been theory suddenly became very real to Mike. He looked at the capsule with a new eye. His turn was coming a week sooner. He was to be the fourth to try the ride—and the first three had been failures.

As for Rod, when he returned to his room to pack, he let go his rage. His cold pale eyes stared around the room in fury and he lashed out suddenly with his foot and kicked the chair. He was so mad he could explode, he thought. Blast that Mike Mars anyway!

He'd have to call Cahoon somehow; he'd have to get still one more Redstone sabotaged. He knew that if the fourth failed, it might indeed cause the whole program to be canceled indefinitely. This might ruin his own chances of following Mike—but, darned if he could see Mike getting away with it!

No, this was the chance to get rid of Mike once and for all. That fourth Redstone had to be tampered with! And then, when Rod himself had flown the X-15, too, he'd be even with Mike—maybe ahead of him, if Mike got hurt in the process.

There wasn't a chance to phone at Skyhook, and he wouldn't have risked it. He looked for the opportunity during the ride to Orlando, but he was hustled onto a waiting Air Force transport too fast to make a call. The ride to California took hours, and it was not until the next day that he managed to reach a private phone out at Edwards where he could call back across the continent to Cahoon. But he was still being thwarted, for his man was never in when he called. He telephoned his father, only to find that the senior Harger was also away on business.

During the next two days, Rod Harger tried again and again to get in touch with the master criminal Cahoon. At last he got him.

Hastily Rod explained what had happened. Cahoon's voice was disturbed, angry. "I can't get in too near that Canaveral operation any more," Cahoon said. "That Mike Mars spotted me there and the alert is on."

"You've got to get through," said Rod furiously. "That fourth shoot must be sabotaged—*must* be!"

"Well," said Cahoon, "seeing as how it's Mike himself that's going to be the victim, I'll make an effort to reach my man at the pad. I don't know—it may be too late—but I'll try."

"See that you do," said Rod. "Everything may depend on it." Rod hung up, mopped his brow. Again he felt so mad that he launched a kick at the side of the telephone booth. He emerged from it, still angry.

"Something wrong, sir?" said an airman who happened to overhear the bang of his foot.

"No, no," Rod snapped, shaking his head and stomping off. In a pig's eye, he thought; everything's getting mixed up.

CHAPTER 16

NO REST FOR A MISSILEMAN

THE DAYS went by with great speed, it seemed to Mike. Only a week, and yet it seemed so short. He was in perfect shape as far as his training was concerned. He'd looked forward to this moment for so long that it seemed to him as if he'd already lived it many times. In his imagination he had.

The new pad was functioning just as well as the old. The crew had simply moved over to the new gantries and the new blockhouse and had gone to work. By now everyone knew his task, and the check-out went along smoothly. Mike visited it twice during that week, watched the operations, talked to the men on the gantry and in the blockhouse. Along with Dr. Van Ness, he had watched while the capsule was hauled up and carefully attached to the nose of the Redstone.

Jethro Manson, the Pad Control Officer, was quiet and rather withdrawn, but he worked skillfully. Mike had occasion to talk to him several times but noticed no reason to be uneasy. In fact, Manson actually was at greater ease this time than he'd been at the last three shoots. The dreadful secret he had held—at the bidding of top-secret authority, as he thought—was off his mind.

So the day dawned for the fourth flight. When Mike came down to breakfast, he was greeted by the other fellows with careful unconcern. As he was eating his eggs, he heard the noise of a wide-open sports-car engine roaring up. He looked up, knowing what was to come. Sure enough, in a few minutes the front door slammed and the slight form of Dr. Van Ness's black-haired daughter came popping into the room.

"Gosh," she said, "just in time for breakfast. I'm so glad I could make it. School's out for the summer, and I just had to get here fast, so I just got up and took off in my car without even waiting for a bite, and I'm just frantic with hunger. Gee, I'm excited, for now I can hang around here and watch all the fun, and I just hate to miss any of it. I just love rockets."

Mike looked up and caught the grinning eyes of his fellow astronauts. "We've got company, looks like," said lanky Jack Lannigan.

As soon as possible, Mike made his getaway, only to be called right back into a quick conference with Dr. Van Ness.

The black-bearded scientist looked him over. "You look fit as a fiddle, Mike," he said. "Not nervous, are you?"

Mike smiled. "No, sir," he said. "I'm ready."

"Well," said Merlin Van Ness, "you won't be needed at the pad until about one o'clock. Report to the locker room at Central Control then; Dr. Holderlin will meet you there. Until then I want you to rest, take it easy, forget everything for the morning. Vivian says she wants to drive down to Cocoa Beach and go swimming. Why not take your own car and go down with her? Get your trunks, get some sunshine, watch the sea gulls."

Mike shrugged. "That doesn't sound bad; guess I'll do it. Where will the other fellows be this shoot?"

"Johnny and Jack will be out on the ship at the landing spot. Williams and Stacey will be in the blockhouse along with me," finished Van Ness.

So it was that in about ten minutes Vivian took off again in her little red car and Mike followed in the blue Air Force car. But just before he left, Johnny got hold of him and they had a brief talk.

It was Johnny Bluehawk's idea that if Cahoon was still trying to do his dirty work, he'd again be out at the beach or near Canaveral that very day. "It's a good chance for you to scout the beach and the town this morning looking for him. I'd suggest you take a weapon."

Mike agreed with this, and when he drove off in the wake of Vivian Van Ness he had his regulation officer's automatic strapped around his waist in its official holster. Besides, he had had a new thought and he meant to carry it through.

They drove down from Skyhook at Vivian's usual fast pace, Mike following sufficiently far behind so as to avoid the dust from the red car ahead. After they had passed through the city of Cocoa and gone across the causeway to the beach below Cape Canaveral, Vivian drew up and waited for him. He drew up alongside her just off the road.

"You go on and drive down to the beach," he said, pointing to the wide sandy road that led straight down to the shore, where the gentle waves of the ocean lapped against the wide, flat expanse of whitish sand. "I've got to go down to the Moonbrite Motel and look up something. I'll be back to meet you by the water in about half an hour."

"All right," said Vivian, "but don't be late. I'm real hungry to get some swimming in, but I'll wait for you. I don't like to go out alone, because sometimes there are jellyfish around and they give me the creeps."

"They make you sick as well," Mike said, "for they're usually the stinging kind."

She waved to him, got in her car and drove down to the beach, parking along the flat hard-packed sand just at the water's edge. Mike drove off.

Cahoon had been having real trouble. After finally getting Rod's phone call and the bad news about the coming fourth flight, he'd tried to call Manson on the phone to give him orders to sabotage. But Manson was busy. The job of being the chief checkout officer right at the rocket itself called for concentration. In the missile field, when a rocket was getting readied, it was often a day-and-night job; and although the Redstone was a relatively simple rocket—not a step rocket—the time given to assemble it was limited and often the work kept Manson overly long at the cape.

Cahoon had called time and again during the next few days and had failed to find the missileman in. Manson's wife didn't know when her husband would be back, and as Cahoon refused to leave either a number Manson could call or his name, the Pad Control Officer just never did know who was calling.

But one morning at last Cahoon rang and Manson's voice answered. Cahoon identified himself, hastily went on: "Our plans have been changed and it is now important that a defect be put into today's rocket shoot. It's not too late. You've got to do it."

Manson was worried, and he said so. "Look, I don't know if I can. There isn't much left to do, and they're suspicious. Are you sure?"

But Cahoon was heated, and he argued, and the more he argued, the more Manson became uneasy. Finally Cahoon coldly informed him that if he didn't do as directed, he'd see to it that it was learned that Manson had done the sabotage. "You'll go to jail if you don't do as I say."

Manson became terrified, for at last he realized that he'd been tricked into something dishonest. Up to then he'd supposed he was working for the government, but now that Cahoon had threatened him that way, he realized what he'd really done. But it was too late, he thought desperately. He was trapped and helpless. He hung up, shaking in fright.

Mike Mars drove to the Moonbrite Motel. It had suddenly occurred to him that there was perhaps one clue left there to the identity of Cahoon's contact at Cape Canaveral. He knew that Air Intelligence had searched the place and found nothing—but maybe they hadn't thought of this angle.

When he reached the motel, he persuaded the manager to let him go to Room 14 again. Fortunately nobody was occupying it that morning. Once inside the room, he took out the telephone directories covering Cocoa Beach and the neighboring towns and systematically began turning the pages, skimming each page rapidly but thoroughly.

He remembered that lots of people, when they call

"You'll do as I say," Cahoon warned.

a new number they've just looked up in the directory, are liable to make a little pencil mark—an X or a check—next to the number in order to dial it right. There was just the possibility that Cahoon might have done this.

He skimmed through page after page. The directory was a thin one, fortunately—and suddenly he stopped. There was a penciled circle around one number.

He looked at the name. Jethro Manson, with a residence right in Cocoa Beach. The name was familiar. Mike quickly ran over the names he knew, and suddenly Manson's face swam into focus. It was the Pad Control Officer!

What better man could be found to sabotage a rocket?

CHAPTER 17

THE SCREAMING GIRL

Mike ran out of the room, raced to his car, and leaped in. He knew that Manson's house was a little ranch-type place right near the causeway road. He turned the car and drove back fast.

As he came to the causeway, he braked to a stop. A man was walking down the beach road, heading for the water. A man who walked stooped over, uncertain, as if deep in thought or sorely troubled. That man was Manson.

Mike turned his car, starting down the beach road slowly, for it was sandy. He stood up in his seat for a moment and called out, "Hey, Manson! Stop!"

The slender, nervous figure stopped and turned around. Mike caught a glimpse of a lined and worried face, a youngish man now torn with anxiety. As soon as Manson saw the familiar shock of Mike Mars's hair, recognized the freckled features of the young fellow in Air Force blue, a look of terror ran across

Manson ran toward Vivian's car.

his face. The missileman turned, started running wildly across the sand.

Mike dropped back into the seat, gunned the engine, and started after him. He was the guilty party all right. He'd get him.

As Manson fled toward the water, hearing the sound of Mike's racing engine, he saw a trim red sports car standing on the sand just by the water. There was a black-haired girl in a bathing suit sitting in it. It was an open car, a sports coupé, and it looked speedy.

Manson ran toward it, and when he reached it he vaulted over its low side and slid into the driver's seat, rudely shoving the girl over. As she screamed, he turned on the ignition and stepped hard on the gas.

The little car jumped forward, turning wildly as Manson twisted the wheel, and then tore along the sandy beach.

Mike saw the thing happen, and even as Manson was gunning the speedy sportster around, Mike had stepped on his own gas, twisting his wheel to follow.

The red car tore along the water-front sand at a rising speed. The sand was flat and hard. The beach was ideal for racing, resembling the famous racing sands at Daytona Beach, only a few dozen miles further to the north. Fortunately, the beach was not crowded yet, as it was too early in the day for bathers to turn up in large groups.

Mike raced his own car after Vivian's, and the two cars roared along the Cocoa Beach water front in a mad, wild chase. First the little red car, with a screaming girl crouched in the front seat, black hair waving wildly in the wind. Then, a couple of dozen yards behind, a blue-gray compact car with a sandy-haired young man in uniform crouched over the wheel.

Probably on a clear driveway the red car would have gotten away easily. But Manson was half out of his mind with terror, the sand was strange, and the sounds of the ocean waves on his left and the screaming girl on his right unnerved him. He didn't quite know how to get the best speed out of the car, and he didn't know where he could go anyway. His only idea, born of desperation, was to get away.

Mike followed with cool determination. He wouldn't let the red car get away. He drew his revolver with his right hand, holding the wheel with his left. He leveled his pistol, then hesitated. Suppose he hit Vivian?

He couldn't chance it. Or could he? He aimed high, fired once. The bullet whined over Manson's head; the report boomed in the desperate man's ear.

He swung the wheel wildly, and the red car twisted and almost turned over. Vivian, screaming louder, grabbed the wheel. Manson struggled with her and, as he did so, his foot came off the gas pedal. The car slowed down.

Mike tore up and, as he neared the careening red car, threw open his own door. As the two cars came side by side, almost at the same speed, he leaped over.

He caught onto the back of the car, pulled himself over the back of the seat, grabbing Manson around the neck. The missileman let go of the wheel with a yell and reached for the choking hands.

Vivian grasped the wheel and held the car steady as it ground to a halt. Manson, pulled half out of the seat, fought vainly for air. Then he suddenly jerked loose, leaped over the side, and ran for the water.

"Stop!" Mike yelled, but the missileman was now

past all understanding. He ran on, as if to drown himself. Mike was still holding his pistol. He leveled it, aimed low, and fired.

Manson threw up his arms, twisted around, fell. The water was low, lapping around him as he lay prone. Mike ran down to him, grabbed his body, and hauled him up onto the dry sand.

The Pad Control Officer was unconscious, whether from shock or from the wound Mike couldn't say. He saw that he'd shot him high in the leg. It couldn't be fatal, but Manson would need medical attention.

A crowd began to gather, for the wild race had attracted attention all up and down the beach. Someone had sent for the local police; someone else had called the Air Force police.

Mike went back to the red car. Vivian jumped out as he approached. "Oh, Mike," she said; "gosh, but you were wonderful! Gee, I was sure I was going to get killed. How did you know to come so quickly? I was never so scared in my life. Who is he? Where are you going? Mike! Come back!"

Mike saw that he was in for some real hero worship and he felt himself getting red. The last thing he wanted was to get kissed in front of the growing crowd. He hastily turned, quickly got back into his car, which had rolled to a stop fifty feet away on the

Mike leveled his pistol and fired.

higher sand. "I'm due at the cape right away," he called to the girl. "Explain everything to the police."

Before she could catch him, he turned the car and drove back up the beach to the causeway.

He'd be early at Central Control, but darned if he wouldn't rather sit around there for a couple hours if he had to. Besides—the question was, had Manson already sabotaged the rocket?

CHAPTER 18

THE TIME IS ZERO

HE WAS early at the green Central Control Building, just as he had thought, but he didn't mind. It seemed to him that it was just as well he wasn't stuck around in a crowd, probably being questioned by the local police. The Project Quicksilver program was still a secret, and it might delay things too long to try to clear up what Manson's motives and crimes had been.

Dr. Holderlin arrived in time to find Mike sitting in the small lunchroom at the main building having a bottle of pop and a sandwich. The twinkling-eyed German space physician slapped him on the back. "You look good and chipper," he said. "I hear you had a little adventure on the sands. You don't feel a little tired from all that exercise?"

Mike grinned. "I feel fine," he said. "I'm ready for a vacation in the beautiful Bahamas. Maybe this afternoon."

Dr. Holderlin chuckled. "O.K. We send you there

right away. Express. By space mail, even yet. So come on with me and we get you into your suit."

Mike got up and the two went on to the room that had been set aside for the astronaut operations. Here a pair of technicians assisted Mike into the pressure suit he would wear in the capsule. It was the same kind of outfit he had worn when flying the X-15, a modified Navy spacesuit, light, with its own heating and cooling system, able to be plugged into the system of the capsule, and holding him as comfortably as a spacesuit would were he standing on the airless surface of the moon. It fit tightly, its silvery reinforced bands clinging to his form. But it was comfortable even if cramped.

They tested the suit carefully, made sure it was all right. Dr. Holderlin took a big white helmet off the shelf, the space helmet, with its wide transparent front visor, that would clamp down completely and close the entire suit off from the outside when ready.

On the front of the helmet someone had been careful to print Mike's own lucky initials—M.A.R.S. —and just above it a little circle with a diagonal arrow jutting from it, the symbol of the planet Mars. Mike took the helmet, held it in his hand.

"Michael Alfred Robert Samson," said Dr. Holderlin slowly, "maybe this is the lucky trip. Just take it easy, keep cool, and we do the trick."

"Keeping cool in this outfit will be a problem on the way to the Redstone pad," Mike remarked lightly. "It's hot outside—Florida-summer hot."

Dr. Holderlin nodded. "We have that licked. That van they use at Edwards, we do not have it here, but we have an air-conditioned car outside and we drive fast. So let's go."

They emerged from the Central Control Building to find a large limousine waiting for them. Entering it, holding his helmet, Mike was grateful for the relief from the hot sun, which had poured its rays on his metallic suit for only a moment. The car drove them quickly away from the green building along the narrow roads between the scrub and underbrush that marked most of the cape. It rapidly crossed the sandy wastes. They came up to the guardhouse, passed through, passed the blockhouse. There were still men in white workmen's helmets on the gantries and before the blockhouse, but the countdown was already in progress. Thin vapors of oxygen were wisping around the base of the tall white-painted Redstone rocket.

Mike got out of the car, conscious again of the hot sun. Assisted by the elderly German, he walked to the open-framed elevator which formed part of the gantry skeleton and rode slowly upward. The elevator came to a stop at the top. He emerged, a shining silver figure, and walked across the narrow platform.

The capsule was waiting. There was a small cluster of workmen around it, obviously waiting for him. Dr. Van Ness was present also, wearing the required crash helmet. As Mike neared the capsule, the bearded scientist came up to him. Mike grinned when he saw that the helmet Van Ness was wearing bore the inscription "Pad Control Officer."

Merlin Van Ness caught his eye, nodded. "It was the only spare helmet around. Manson won't need it any more." He held out his hand, grasped Mike's, shook it quickly. "Thanks, Mike, a father's thanks."

Mike flushed slightly. "It wasn't anything, sir," he said. "Did Manson say anything about this rocket, sir?" he added quickly.

"He hasn't regained consciousness yet," Van Ness said. "We don't know whether this Redstone has been tampered with. We think not, but we don't know for sure." He paused, then went on. "Mike, if you want us to, we'll put a hold on this countdown, set it back twenty-four hours, and run a complete check again."

Mike shook his head. "No, no. I'll take my chances. I think maybe the dirty work was to be done at the last minute, and I don't want to delay any longer."

Merlin Van Ness glanced at the capsule just in front of them. It stood atop the rocket, orange-painted, with a bright-red tower at the top—the sixteen-foot tower that held the special escape rocket that could take the capsule to safety in the event of an emergency during the rise. Mike hoped it wouldn't be needed this time.

Without saying more, he walked over to the capsule. Assisted personally by Van Ness and Holderlin, he bent down and squeezed through the tight space of the hatch near the top of the capsule. He slid back into the astronaut's seat.

It was a deep contour chair, molded to fit his body exactly, and it held him with complete protection along the back and sides of his body. Mike had tested this seat many times, and as he slid into it and adjusted himself it seemed to him that this was just another maneuver. He was in a sitting position, except that he was on his back, with his feet raised up and the backs of his arms resting against the seat.

He closed his helmet and turned on the suit's self-ventilating system. He plugged in his various suit elements to those of the capsule. He looked around.

It was cramped, very cramped. It was like being sealed up in a can. The hatch had been fitted back into place and sealed. Just before him was the gleaming panel of the instrument board, within reach of his hands without his having to lift his elbows. Above was a wide window through which he could see the sky and the framework of the upper gantry as well as catch a glimpse of the framework of the escape rocket rising atop. With a touch of his finger on the panel he could bring a periscope into play and get a view of the ground below him.

He knew the capsule well and had faith in it. It had stood up under many hard tests. It had stood up under three emergency Redstone decisions. Its body was light, made of titanium, with a double-skin, braced and insulated. It should be sufficient to ward off the dangers of outer space, the cold and the heat, the airlessness, and even what radiation might be present at the level he would rise to.

"T minus forty and counting," said a voice in his earphones, the same voice he had heard last week in the other blockhouse. Forty minutes to go, well, that wasn't so bad.

The time passed quickly enough. He listened to the countdown proceed, answered the queries concerning him, ran a quick test over his own instruments. He knew the capsule was fully automatic, that it could be directed by radio from the ground if anything failed. Actually he was a passenger this time, and his duties as pilot would come up only if some-

The time is zero!

thing failed. Nothing should, he knew. His job was to observe.

"T minus six minutes," came the voice. Mike thought again of Manson. Had this rocket been sabotaged also? Would there come a moment of shock and then—sudden disaster? How could they tell?

He stared up through the window. The gantry was being withdrawn; he saw its upper framework disappear from his view. He heard the countdown come to five minutes, then to three, to one. He smiled suddenly and said softly to himself:

> Michael Mars is my name.
> America's my nation.
> Space-flying is my game
> And Mars my destination!

"T minus ten seconds," said the voice at last. Mike tightened his lips, took a deep breath. "Five, four, three, two, one, zero," counted off the calm tones of the talker.

From somewhere below there came a faint rumbling vibration.

CHAPTER 19

VISION OF VENUS

AT FIRST Mike felt nothing, and he knew that the rocket was straining to lift itself from its pad. Then as the seconds moved by and the rumbling continued from below, he felt himself sinking slowly back into his seat. Still nothing much, but the pressure was rising as the rocket was forcing itself up.

He watched the dials carefully, watching the time and the altimeter. It must be a foot up now, on its roaring, raging clouds of flaming gas. And at that point he felt the pressure on his body beginning to grow slowly.

The rocket was moving upward, faster and faster, and as it accelerated, the pressure on him grew. He was calm, cool, as he always was.

Below him the Redstone gathered momentum; now it must be standing on a cloud of gas as long as itself. Now it must be higher than the gantry tops.

Mike knew that it would soon be visible from the cape and from the beaches.

Somewhere there would be a red car and a gabby girl watching on a beach, and somewhere else there would be a tense, angry figure, with a faint hooked scar, watching. Cahoon must be seeing this, Mike thought. Would he be waiting for an explosion that he alone would think was coming—or would he be clenching his teeth in frustrated fury when he realized the plan might fail?

The pressure was growing greater, and Mike felt himself being pressed down in his contour chair as if by a giant hand. He was crushed back, his head and his body pressed against the yielding surface of the remarkable, form-fitting seat. In his ears he could hear the talker's voice counting out the seconds that had passed since the firing.

But the sound of the voice was being drowned out now by a throbbing in his ears, a thrumming of blood from the pressure. He fought for breath as the pressure grew with alarming rapidity. Three G's, four, five, six; he saw the meter on his instrument board swimming before his eyes and saw its G dial moving steadily over. Each G was a doubling of his own weight, each G made his body heavier, made his muscles work under more and more terrible burdens.

Eight, nine G's, and the meter rested. His eyes felt

Mike felt as if he were being crushed by a giant hand.

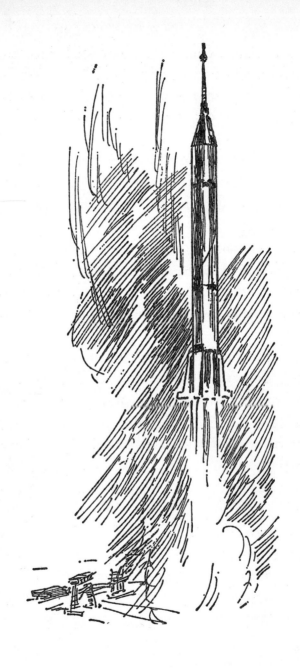

as if a giant's thumbs were pressed into them. His lips fell back and he couldn't pull them over his bared teeth. His cheeks were drawn in, his breath forced out of his lungs as his ribs seemed about to cave in.

Not for long, he thought to himself. I can stand this. He held on, forcibly moved his fingers with tremendous effort. His eyes, unable to blink, looked out the reinforced window. He saw sky, blue sky, and nothing else.

The pressure remained constant for a while, and he was conscious of the rumbling roaring of the rocket engine beneath him. He tried to squirm but couldn't. Time, time . . . how long were just a few seconds under that strain!

Then it suddenly stopped. Broke off, cut out. The gauge dropped, he was rising, racing upward atop a rocket into the upper atmosphere, and the rocket had burned out its fuel, had sent him upward on the required momentum. The rest of the way would be coasting.

He felt light, but the pressure was not entirely off. He was held by the gravity of the Earth, still on him as he rose, but he was comfortable again. A voice sounded in his ear. "Capsule report, please."

He spoke, "Capsule reporting. All O.K."

He almost imagined he could hear a sigh of relief

in his earphones. They were tense there, too. Somehow now he didn't feel tense at all. He felt happy.

He watched his instruments. There was an audible click above him. He looked upward through his viewplate. The red sixteen-foot tower of his emergency rocket seemed to slide away from view; it was torn off; it vanished. Forty miles up, Mike thought, and there's no need for the emergency escape system now.

The rocket would be rising fast, and he waited for the next change.

It came with a sudden bump, a shove from underneath. That was an explosion, Mike thought, and immediately understood it. It was the charge that separated the capsule from the now empty and useless Redstone rocket. The capsule was on its own now, rolling through the sky on its individual orbit, while the towering tube of the burned-out rocket would go its way, rise, and then fall, shattered and in flames, into the ocean.

Seventy miles up then, Mike figured.

He looked through his window. He could see the ocean, a blue, gleaming mass, and at its edge the greenish-yellow of the Florida coast. He could see the whole of Florida, outlined clearly as if in a geography book, and there were little fluffs of mist along one edge of it, and, beyond, the shining surface of the Gulf of Mexico. He rose slightly, shifted his view.

The top of Cuba, the steps of the Keys, all were there.

The sky was dark blue, getting darker steadily. Ninety miles now and still rising. The capsule was tipping slightly, not much, and he could see the darkening expanse of the Atlantic Ocean spreading out below and the dark line where the night was coming, spreading out across the horizon. The Earth was beginning to look like a planet. He could see the curving horizon following the edge of twilight.

The capsule was slowing on its own momentum now, and Mike worked his periscope to see below him, but there was gleaming ocean and the geography again. He felt good.

As he rose he talked, answering the questions from the blockhouse now so far away. Dr. Van Ness's voice came on, asking for descriptions of the scene. And Dr. Holderlin now and then asked how he felt.

"I feel fine," Mike said. "I have a feeling—as if I'm cramped in—a man in a can—but it's strangely comfortable."

His weight steadily dropped as the capsule arched into its curve and drew away from the Earth. Then came the moment, one hundred and twenty miles up, when his weight finally came to zero.

He was too snug to be able to rise and float around, but he knew the sensation. He had experienced it for measured seconds in special flights. He had experienced it for minutes at the height of his X-15 flight. Now he experienced it again.

For Mike, being weightless was a very pleasing sensation. He felt happy, almost giddy. For others he knew it could be as upsetting as seasickness, but the astronauts, like most airplane pilots, did not experience that kind of trouble. Mike liked the sensation of feeling that he could float around like a bubble. He could let his hand rise and just let it hang in the air.

"No ill effects," he reported in answer to a query from the German scientist. "Outside it's quite dark, night time again, though I can see the sun off in the west. Quite a corona display, too. I hope the cameras catch it."

"Stars out?" said Van Ness's voice.

Mike looked out the window. It was night black outside. The stars? Yes, they were out, and many of them. He described what he saw, and . . . there was one low in the east, shining, white, and slightly crescent.

"Venus is terrific," Mike said. "I can see it as a crescent here without a telescope. Almost makes me feel as if I could reach out and take it."

"Soon enough," said Van Ness's voice dryly. "Before you know it."

CHAPTER 20

OUT OF THE SKY

"Get ready for the descent," cut in the calm tones of someone, possibly in the Central Control Building at Canaveral. For an instant Mike became aware of how many people were listening in to him, measuring his ride. Stations at the cape, stations out at sea and on the islands of the Atlantic Missile Test Range— all were riding mentally at his side.

Mike felt that his weight was returning, and he saw from his instruments that his five minutes in free flight were at an end. The hardest part of the trajectory was coming. He set himself back again, prepared.

The capsule came down, and as it came the rising number of air particles as the atmosphere grew thicker began to rub against the outer metal skin of the space can. This friction began to raise the temperature. The outer shell got hot.

There were two layers of metal skin inside the capsule. It was insulated, and still the question remained as to how well it would hold up. Mike watched the outer skin temperature indicator with concern. It was getting hotter, red hot by now, and within he could see that the inner skin was rising fast.

His personal cooling system worked all right. The suit kept him comfortable but, inside, the air of the capsule was up to ninety and rising slowly. Mike quickly figured the time left and decided he'd make it.

The capsule was falling; then there was a shock beneath him. The pressure rose underneath as the retro-rockets built into the base went automatically into action. Their discharge slowed down the falling capsule and brought it down to the speed that would make it possible to land without burning up altogether.

Outside the sky had lightened; he could still see Florida, but it was bigger and drawing away from his view. He could see specks of green islands coming into the edge of his eastern vision.

"Riding down on schedule," Mike called out. He heard a voice check this.

The rockets stopped. There was a momentary pause, a feeling of sheer dropping again, an instant of no gravity, and then something blossomed above him, filling for a split second the window view.

It was the small drogue parachute, designed to

check the initial fall and then pull out and open the big chute. There was another click above him, and his window was filled with the orange-and-white-striped folds of the big parachute. It spread out, held, umbrellaed over him. The capsule began to slow, began to drag and twist beneath the air-filled folds of the huge chute.

Mike looked out. The water was in view; he could see the surface a mile below him now. He lay back in his seat and enjoyed the last minutes of the fall. The capsule swayed beneath the parachute like the basket of a balloon.

"You're in sight, Mike," said a familiar voice—that of Colonel Drummond. The colonel was out on the rescue ship just off Grand Bahama Island. Johnny Bluehawk would be there, too, and tall Jack Lannigan as well.

Mike smiled to himself now. The capsule swung about, and then the ocean seemed to come up sharp and fast.

He saw the waves, he saw the water, and then there was a sharp thump on the capsule. The water closed over the window and for a few seconds all he could see were the blue-green depths.

The capsule popped up again, bounced a little on the waves, then began a gentle swaying as it rocked.

Mike squirmed around and looked about him.

There was a slapping, thumping sound. What was that? He searched the narrow space. Nothing. Oh— it was the waves pounding the outside of the bobbing can.

Time to get out, he thought. He unstrapped himself from the contour couch, unplugged the ventilator that kept his suit part of the capsule's internal system. He reached out and uncoupled part of the instrument panel, swung it aside. Reaching behind the panel, he found the pressure hatch.

Mike loosened it, pulled it out, and dropped it beside him. He stood up and shoved himself inside the narrow neck of the capsule. It was still tight and dark. He reached up and found the canister that had held the parachutes. He pulled out the restraining pins, ripped off a couple of wires.

Reaching back into the body of the capsule, Mike got hold of his emergency pack and, holding it in one hand, shoved outward again. The canister fell away and the hatch was open. The outer air came in.

Mike squirmed through the narrow opening, pushed his pack out before him, and activated it. The pack's rubber raft bounced out, inflated itself rapidly, even as Mike was squeezing through the bottleneck of the bobbing, floating capsule.

He pulled himself all the way, slipped into the water, grabbed the raft, and pulled himself on it.

Mike squirmed out of the capsule.

He sat up, opened his helmet plate, and took deep breaths of the fresh, warm ocean air. Then he looked around.

Coming up to him, about a hundred feet away, was the prow of a white naval vessel, a small ship like the rescue ships that operated around the cape. Hanging over the rail at the bow, waving to him as they drew closer, were Johnny and Jack. He could make out their laughing features, and he could see the now equally radiant face of the commander of the Quicksilver astronauts, Colonel Drummond.

Mike Mars waved back at them, conscious that he had taken yet another step up the ladder into space. This was a big one—the first man to ride a rocket and to test out an actual space cabin. The next step would come very soon after, he thought—the first manned flight in space around the world. There had to be a satellite with a man like himself in it. That would be an adventure, Mike thought, and he wondered how it would turn out.

C20